LOVE, SHIPS & SEA SERPENTS

Elaine Canyon

LOVE, SHIPS & SEA SERPENTS

For information contact:

Elaine Canyon
https://elainecanyon.com

Cover Design: GetCovers
Formatting: Elaine Canyon

ISBN: 978-1-963576-08-5 (bespoke hbk.) — ISBN: 978-1-963576-07-8 (hbk.) — ISBN: 978-1-963576-01-6 (pbk.) — ISBN: 978-1-963576-00-9 (ebook)

First Edition: March 2024
Updated: September 2025

10 9 8 7 6 5 4 3 2 1

To my husband,
who first told me I needed to shift from
only writing fanfiction to
writing original fiction, too.
You were right. ♥

Chapter One

Dying Would Be A Major Inconvenience

Hannah leaned over the railing of *The Siren's* main deck, getting close enough for the spray of the Sea to cool her from the unusual noon heat, breathing in the brisk salted air and tasting the brine. From this angle, she blocked what they were chasing from view and could focus on how the sun was scorching her.

Of the Three Sisters—creators of the world and all its creatures—Hannah wondered which was in charge of the weather. Likely, the Sky controlled the weather, but Hannah wouldn't be surprised to find out that the Sea did. As a human, Hannah ought to ask Mother Land to take care of the heat that beat down on them, but Hannah Vallens had grown up with more allegiance to the Sea than the Sister that had created her.

"Debating a swim?" Nicholas Ainsley's voice sounded behind her.

"The Sea is much cooler than the deck of this ship." Hannah smiled and pushed off the railing.

Nicholas barked a laugh and brushed his dirty blonde hair from his pale blue eyes. Hannah ignored the butterflies that fluttered in her stomach. She'd spent ten years developing the skill of ignoring the butterflies Nicholas gave her and was rather proficient at it.

At least, she hoped she was. Nicholas gave no indication he saw her as anything more than a sister, no matter how much she wished it were otherwise.

"Probably not worth getting left behind." Nicholas slid up next to her, leaning against the railing as his large frame mercifully shadowed her from the sun. "Especially with how we're gaining on them." He pointed at the Nerland naval ship they were chasing.

Hannah's relief from Nicholas's shadow slipped away as she reluctantly turned to where he pointed. What had started as a black dot on the horizon now was a ship the size of her forearm. The irony of chasing and sinking ships from the country she was born to wasn't lost on Hannah. But the irony didn't change that the sailors on any Nerland naval ship would kill her if given half a chance. If they could prove every member of *The Siren's* crew was dead, their king would reward that ship's captain with a duchy.

"Why do we always cross paths with those ships right before meals?" Hannah turned back to Nicholas, gripping the railing in an attempt to transfer her nervous energy to the smooth wood beneath her fingers.

"I bet Corny Junior harbors a witch in his castle. Their sole job is to control enough spirits to keep chasing after us. Then the navy can send ships to intercept our path right before lunch." Nicholas bumped her shoulder and chuckled. "Don't worry. We'll sink them and then you can join the lunch preparations."

"Aye, but I don't think Corny Junior would employ a witch." Hannah shoved back against him, ignoring the hope in her heart that he'd wrap his arm around her shoulders. Instead, she focused on the reason they were chasing this ship. Killing men was always easier when she remembered why she was doing it.

Corny Junior, King Cornelius II of Nerland, was the son of the king that drove *The Siren's* crew out of the country twenty-five years ago. If things had gone differently, Hannah would have been the daughter of Duke David Vallens and Duchess Alice Vallens. And dead. Instead, James and Maggie Roberts saved Hannah's family and five other noble families that King Cornelius I ordered to be executed. Now they lived on *The Siren* and a hidden island in the Mer Sea, spending their lives sinking Nerland naval ships before the Nerlanders could sink *The Siren*. Apparently, a duchy was a decent enough reward for so many of them to wind up on the ocean floor.

"You're probably right." Nicholas wrapped his arm around her shoulders and Hannah held back the happy sigh that tried to escape her lips. "I bet the coward fears witches."

"He would be one to make them angry." Hannah nodded with a smile and curled further under Nicholas's arm, wishing that the Sea would swallow up the Nerland ship they were chasing. Then she could spend the day right here instead of taking an hour or two fighting for her life. Maybe if the ship's spotter, Anthony, asked the Sea with a bit of sweetness and flattery, she'd oblige him.

At a year older than her, the same as Nicholas, Anthony was the closest thing Hannah had to a brother. While his parents were the reason *The Siren's* crew made it out of Nerland alive, Anthony was the reason they were still breathing.Anthony possessed an ability no human should have.

He could speak to the Sea.

And the Sea answered.

At a year old, his ability kept the Merfolk from sinking *The Siren* on sight, as was their custom for every other ship that entered the Mer Sea. According to both Anthony and Hannah's mermaid friends, because of Anthony's ability, the Sea had commanded them to give the crew safe passage and protection.

But their protection came at a price.

To protect themselves from the humans that hunted mermaids for sport, the Merfolk wouldn't allow any new crew members to join *The Siren*. That included children being born into the crew. Those who stayed on the ship were barren until they gave up the protection of the Merfolk to permanently live on Mother Land.

Never to return to *The Siren*.

The lump in Hannah's throat tried to suffocate her as she pushed back the reminder that she would never have children of her own if she stayed. And if she left, she'd lose

Nicholas from her life. Neither path gave her a life in calm waters.

"We're getting closer. Captain's going to call out orders soon." Nicholas's hand slid against the loose fabric of her sleeve. "Are you ready?"

Hannah focused on his touch, distracting herself from her internal agony. "As ready as I can be." She was tired of fighting, both Nerlanders and herself.

Captain Roberts's whistle cut through her thoughts as he called out orders.

"If you need me, just holler." Nicholas squeezed her shoulders once before moving for his parents. Matthew Ainsley and his wife Rebecca would need Nicholas's help to get the cannons in position. They only had a few more minutes before the fighting would start.

Hannah set her shoulders and looked at the approaching Nerland ship. It and its crew would sit at the bottom of the ocean in the next hour. They had to.

She couldn't make lunch until they did.

The fighting started innocently enough, at least until the Nerland ship pulled in too close and a couple dozen Nerland sailors swung from the ropes to *The Siren's* decks.

So much for sinking them quickly and getting on to making lunch.

Hannah engaged another sailor, shoving him back and taking advantage of his misstep on the deck. The Sea rocked beneath *The Siren*, throwing the Nerland sailor off balance further and over the railing. Hannah offered a silent thanks to the Sea as she watched the man swallowed up in the waves.

If she couldn't have lunch, she could ensure the monsters beneath the surface had a decent spread for their midday meal. For now, she'd make do with the taste of gunpowder in the air.

She didn't have long to contemplate which monsters might enjoy raw Nerlander as another sailor ran towards her from the forecastle deck. Hannah set her shoulders and ran forward past several crew members engaged in similar scuttles defending the cannons. She ignored the sweat dripping down her face and launched herself toward her attacker, dodging his strike and sinking her sword through his chest. The man's weight and momentum knocked her off balance, and Hannah spun to ensure he'd land beneath her. They hit with a thud, Hannah's shoulder smacking the railing, but she thanked Mother Land that her fast thinking kept her from getting crushed under the corpse. She scrambled to her feet and tried to free the blade from the man's chest.

It wouldn't budge.

Of course it wouldn't.

Her frustration as she struggled with the sword morphed to panic when she caught sight of a third Nerland sailor stalking towards her. She hadn't had time to reload her flintlock pistol, and now her sword was stuck. A quick look around her proved that every crew member on the main deck was engaged with their own attackers.

What a wretched day. How had she gone from trying not to be obvious about getting Nicholas to wrap his arm around her to having her sword stuck in an idiot's chest?

Desperate to buy herself some time, Hannah hefted the body attached to her hilt up from the deck. The cannons fired, rocking the ship and aiding in lifting the dead weight until it rested against her. The awful smell of blood and sweat filled her nostrils, and Hannah did her best to keep her breakfast in her stomach as she set her feet. She'd meet her attacker head on and, Mother Land willing, dislodge her sword. That or the corpse might keep the oncoming attack from being fatal. Living and injured was better than dying. Probably. Dirty blonde hair flashed above her and a familiar battle cry sounded through the cotton in her ears as a figure flipped from the forecastle behind her. Nicholas landed on the approaching sailor, his boot dagger pressing into her attacker's neck.

"All right, Hannah?" Nicholas shouted as he jumped up and grabbed the body stuck on her sword, taking the weight from her.

"Aye, thanks to you," Hannah yelled back and braced her foot against the dead sailor, wrenching her sword free.

"What are friends for?" Nicholas tossed the body aside and grinned at her with the smile that always made her think he was keeping a secret from her. "After all, you dying would majorly inconvenience the lunch preparations when this is over."

He drew his sword and sliced open the back of a sailor trying to jump overboard, sending the man screaming over the railing.

Nicholas winked at her. "Now the sharks know there's food down there."

The Sea heaved beneath them, rocking *The Siren* and throwing Hannah into Nicholas. His free arm squeezed around her back, pressing their chests together. For a moment, Hannah forgot they were in the middle of fighting for their lives. This was the dream. To live a life where no one tried to kill her and she could curl into Nicholas's arm whenever she wanted.The blissful moment evaporated as Hannah caught sight of a Nerland sailor running at them from behind Nicholas. She didn't think as she shoved Nicholas around her. Her sword crashed with the Nerlander's before it could come down on Nicholas's head.

Steel crashed behind her, and Nicholas's back left hers. Hannah assured herself Nicholas would be fine and focused on defending against the sailor in front of her. Ignoring the surrounding fighting kept her alive, but it always left a bitter taste in her mouth. The crew was her family, and while none of them had been killed since they left Nerland, she still worried each battle would break their streak.

Hannah forced her attacker around towards the steps to the forecastle and, with a quick parry, caught his sword arm to kick his feet out from under him. This time, her sword didn't get caught as she killed yet another Nerlander, shoving him over the railing and into the Sea.

She turned to see Nicholas pull his sword from his attacker's side before grabbing the man by his shirt and tossing him overboard.

"Well done there." He wiped his shirtsleeve across his forehead. "I'll be sure to—"

A sharp whistle cut him off. Captain Roberts's order to sail on startled the last of the Nerland sailors still aboard *The Siren*. A few final screams filtered through her cottoned ears as her crewmates made sure no Nerlanders would sail on with them.

"Let's go." Nicholas took her hand in a firm grip that sent waves through her arm as they ran for the rigging at the mainmast.

She didn't have time to dwell on the enchanting feeling as they reached the ropes and Nicholas, regrettably, let her go.

The Siren's cannons fired once more, and the ship heaved as they pulled away. Hannah looked up from the rigging and watched as the attacking ship started its final descent beneath the Sea's waves.

The monsters would have another crew of Nerlanders.

"All right, Hannah?" Nicholas's warm voice pulled her attention back from the sinking ship. His musky odor filled her nostrils as he spoke next to her ear. She wanted to lean into him, instead she pulled the cotton from her ears and yanked on the ropes.

"Aye, but I hate when they board us."

"Makes it easier to sink them." Nicholas bumped her shoulder with his, his voice no longer muffled. "But I get it. Even after all this time, it's unnerving watching them swing onto our decks."

It was. Hannah wished she hadn't been one of the youngest of *The Siren's* crew of disgraced Nerlander nobility. Maybe then she would be among those who left *The Siren* for port cities and started families years ago, before she ever fell for Nicholas.

"Maybe someday we won't have to worry about it." She tied off the ropes and rested her hip against the railing. The sun beat down on her and she pulled a drink from her waterskin, wishing the water were still cool.

"I guess Corny Junior could drop dead at any moment," Nicholas laughed. "Till then, I'll keep my sword sharp."

"Have you ever thought of it?" Hannah bit her lip as she broached her most plaguing thought. "A life on Mother Land?"

Her thoughts turned to their recent visit to one of the crew members who'd left for a life on Mother Land, her friend Edith. Holding Edith's new baby had both cut holes in Hannah's heart and filled her with joy. Of the entire crew, current members and those that had left, Edith was the only one who knew that Hannah wanted children of her own. And during this visit, Edith privately offered Hannah a home with her if she ever wanted a life on Mother Land, too.

"This ship won't have enough people to keep sailing if more of us leave." Nicholas shook his head. "Even if I wanted to, I wouldn't put the crew, or the crew members that have left *The Siren*, in that kind of danger. The Merfolk would think we didn't need the protection if enough left that we couldn't man the ship. And I can't see them changing their rules and letting us bring anyone new on."

He was wrong about *The Siren* still sailing. One person could leave and the crew would be enough to sail her. But Nicholas was right about the Merfolk. Hannah loved the Merfolk, she couldn't ask them to put their species in danger for her sake.

"Maybe Corny Junior would believe that we all perished in a storm." Hannah finally responded.

"If he's anything like the stories that our folks tell about his father, then I wouldn't count on it. He'd want proof that we were all dead, just like his father did when he was Nerland's king. And that could lead these same men attacking us to go searching the ports we frequent to ensure every last crew member is dead, including the ones who've already left us."

"And their new families." Hannah's heart clenched. She'd sworn while holding Edith's baby girl that no Nerlander would ever touch her. She couldn't let anything happen to her, or any of the other children born to old crew members.

"Exactly." Nicholas said. "As long as *The Siren* sails, no one will think that we've had people leave. No one will have reason to go looking for our crew members anywhere else."

He made it sound so cut and dry, and Hannah supposed it was. But there was one part to all of it that didn't seem to concern Nicholas. Staying on *The Siren* protected the crew, and it ensured Nicholas stayed in her life, but Hannah would never have children of her own. And that reality threatened to undo her faster than this blasted heat wave.

"You two all right?" Anthony jumped the last several steps from the quarterdeck and came to stand next to Hannah at the railing. His dark hair curled with sweat, sticking to his tanned forehead.

"Aye, though Hannah tried to decorate her hilt with a dead Nerlander."

"Even the Sea will tell you that's an ugly choice, Hannah." Anthony teased her.

"Shove off both of you!" Hannah crossed her arms and bit her lip to hide her smile.

"Don't be like that." Nicholas wrapped his arm around her shoulders and Hannah couldn't suppress her smile any longer.

Anthony threw his arm around her as well, the three of them facing the Sea as *The Siren* glided through the water.

"Aye, the Sea finds beauty in all sorts of things that I find repulsive. Leviathans, for example, are hideous to me, but she insists that they're darlings."

"You should ask the Sea to find you a beautiful creature to spend your life with." Hannah dished back. "I'm sure there's a sea serpent that would love to curl up with you."

"Har, har, har." Anthony moved his arm off her shoulders.

Hannah rested her head on Nicholas's shoulder before he, too, could pull his arm away.

"I'm going to see what Captain wants done next." Anthony turned and headed towards where his father, Captain Roberts, stood with several of the crew.

"If he's taking suggestions, my vote is lunch!" Nicholas called after him.

Hannah seconded his suggestion. Food and drink sounded better at the moment than a nap on the beach of their protected island in the Mer Sea.

"About what you said earlier." Nicholas squeezed her shoulders and Hannah wished for the millionth time that things could be different between them. "Is it really so bad to be stuck with us?

"A rag-tag bunch of pirates? I suppose I could do worse." Hannah gave him a sad smile before she turned toward the Sea.

"What about our pact with Anthony?" Nicholas's fingers slid down her arm to her elbow and back up to her shoulder, sending tides across her skin.

"Do you not want to take over the ship when his parents are ready to retire?"

"I'm not saying that I've changed my mind." Hannah closed her eyes, seeing Edith's baby in her arms again. "I guess when we visited Edith, I thought that life looked kind of nice."

It would be even nicer if she could have that life with a specific dirty blonde hair, blue-eyed pirate, but he just told her he wouldn't leave *The Siren*.

"We get that life when we go back to the island." Nicholas's voice had gone quiet, and his answer told her he misunderstood what she wanted from Edith's life. "Maybe you're feeling waterlogged, and this heat isn't helping any of us. And who knows, perhaps one day we'll stop joking about killing Corny ourselves. But we'll be back on Mother Land within the month. I'm sure after a day or two you'll feel better."

She wouldn't, though. She wasn't yet twenty-five, but Hannah was realizing she wanted more from her life than sailing the Sea, attacking Nerland naval ships, and defending against Nerland bounty hunters. Things like a husband, children of her own, not having to fight for her life so often, felt more important—and unattainable—with each passing day.

"Aye." Hannah lied. "You're probably right."Captain Roberts's whistle blew for the day to resume to normal. Time to prepare a rather late lunch.At least she was alive to do so.

"That's me." Hannah reluctantly pulled out from under Nicholas's arm. "I'll see you at lunch."

"Here." He stepped up behind her, lifting her arm before reaching around and taking hold of the belt that held her scabbard. He slid her pistol from the belt before his deft fingers undid the buckle, taking the sheathed sword from her waist. Hannah's heart shook like cannon fire in her chest at how close he was. If she turned her head, her lips would graze his neck, but she forced herself to remain still.

"I'll sharpen your sword and clean your pistol while you make lunch." He stepped back and Hannah's breath followed him.

"Father will say you're spoiling me again." She cleared her throat, trying to gain some substance behind her voice as she turned to face him. "David has been telling me that for ten years now, and you still don't look spoiled." Nicholas smirked and leaned in next to her ear before sniffing until he snorted. Hannah shrieked and cringed away from him as she laughed.

"Get off!"

"You still don't smell spoiled, either." He tucked her pistol into his belt. "Sneak me something sweet from the galley and I'll call us even."

"Fine." Hannah smiled despite the melancholy pushing at her. This was why she hadn't jumped at Edith's offer to leave *The Siren* and start a new life. A life without Nicholas wasn't one she was sure she could survive. She needed his smiling face and his ability to make her smile when she had no reason to do so. "Know that if I get caught, I'll make you answer to Maggie."

"Maggie's soft on us and you know it. Anthony would perish without his two best friends, and she won't risk her son's happiness."

"But she might make us swab the deck three turns in a row."

"As long as I'm doing it with you, it'll be all right." He winked at her and started towards the weapon stores. "I'll have these back to you by evening."

Hannah smiled as he walked away, but Edith's offer still echoed in her mind.

She wanted children more than anything.

Anything except a life without Nicholas.

If only he'd leave with her.

Hannah swallowed back the tears. She needed to make her choice, but it certainly didn't need to be before she'd had lunch. With a steadying breath, Hannah set her shoulders and descended the steps into the oppressive heat below deck. Being stuck in the galley in this heat was going to be awful.

Perhaps she would have been better off jumping into the Sea before the Nerlanders attacked after all.

Chapter Two
(Trying To) Never Surrender

Stars sparkled above *The Siren* as the crew enjoyed the evening's entertainment on the main deck. After sinking Nerlanders, the crew preferred music and dancing. Normally, Nicholas enjoyed these celebratory evenings, but right now, he wished it was anything but dancing.

Nicholas breathed in the night's cool air, captivated as Hannah spun in her father's arms near the mainmast. Nicholas hid at the railing in the shadows near the stairs to the quarterdeck, enthralled by how Hannah's brown braid caught the torchlight and reflected red back at him. It fit her, red. Hannah was red in the way she fought, the way she teased, the way she never stood by, always pushing for what she wanted.

That last trait scared him right now.

Nicholas's earliest memories included Hannah pushing until she got what she wanted. At eleven-years-old, Hannah had wanted to prove she was better with a dagger than Nicholas and Anthony. He hadn't thought much of it, but Hannah had thrown herself into practicing. When she finally challenged him and Anthony — without any of the older crew members around to stop them—she cut his right bicep deep enough he still bore a scar. Hannah had mellowed with age, but that hadn't dampened her determination. It was there when she ran her sword through an attacker; when she worked their chores on *The Siren*; when she tried her best not to laugh at the things he did specifically to draw a smile from her. And he'd seen that same determination in her brown eyes this afternoon as she'd talked about a life away from *The Siren*.

She wanted that life.

And he would lose her if she found it.

"Are you all right?"

Nicholas jumped and turned to Anthony. "Sea and Sky, Anthony, warn a man."

Anthony grinned. "I figured you'd expect me to come over when I stopped playing."

Nicholas turned to where his mother and other crew members played music near the forecastle deck. Anthony's pipes lay on his empty stool.

"You didn't notice I stopped playing, did you?" Anthony ribbed him.

"I'm thinking." Nicholas snapped and looked back at Hannah. He loved Anthony, but his friend rarely realized when he was pushing too far.

"I only meant to tease."

Nicholas cringed at the hurt in Anthony's voice. "Sorry. I've got a problem, and I'm trying to figure it out. I didn't mean to be curt."

"Let me help then." Anthony leaned back on the railing behind them and handed Nicholas a bari stick before taking out a second and biting down on it. "And what have you been staring at all evening?"

"Nothing." Nicholas tore his eyes from Hannah and bit down hard on the bari stick, hoping the citrus flavor would keep him distracted.

Anthony raised his eyebrows at him, slipping the fibrous stick from his mouth. "I'm pretty sure Hannah would run you through for calling her nothing."

Nicholas's face burned. He'd put in a lot of effort over the last ten years to not get caught staring at Hannah. Staring at her was as much a part of him as his sword hand, but he hid it well. At least, he had, until now.

"Why are you staring at Hannah?" Anthony bit back down on his bari stick and crossed his arms.

That was the question, wasn't it? One Nicholas wasn't sure he could bring himself to answer aloud. Hannah was everything, though he had never verbalized that fact. But Anthony was practically his brother. If Nicholas couldn't trust Anthony, could he claim to trust anyone else?

"I can't help that I stare at her, and believe me, I've tried." He bit harder on the stick, a fresh wave of flavor filling his mouth.

"That's fantastic!" Anthony clapped him on the shoulder. "When were you going to tell me the two of you were taking the waves together?"

"No." Nicholas rubbed his hands over his face and pulled the bari stick from his mouth. "It's not like that. She doesn't know that I..." he trailed off.

"That you like her as more than our surrogate sister? Tell her, then. I'm certain she feels the same." Anthony flipped his bari stick around and bit down with a grin.

"It's not that simple."

"Of course it is. You can't know if she feels the same if you don't tell her."

Nicholas bit back his frustrated retort, chewing instead on the bari stick till the fibers began separating. He spit the stick into the waves and brought Anthony in on his inner turmoil.

"If she has it in her head to leave, then it won't matter what I tell her."

Anthony shoved off of the railing, his bari stick falling from his mouth, and he caught it just before it hit the deck. "What do you mean, leave?"

"She told me before lunch today that life on Mother Land looked appealing." Nicholas's opinion on the matter mirrored Anthony's look of shock and dismay.

"Why in Sky's name would she want to leave *The Siren*? Leave us?" Anthony's bari stick hung between his fingers, dripping saliva onto the deck.

"I think it came about after seeing how happy Edith was when we visited her."

Anthony swore and chucked his bari stick into the Sea.

Nicholas agreed, but privately, he didn't blame Hannah. Seeing Edith's quiet life on Mother Land,

Nicholas couldn't deny that he wanted that life, too. But that option was out for him and he knew it. While *The Siren* could lose one more crew member and manage all right, he wouldn't, couldn't, leave. *The Siren* was his home and the only family he could have. His parents were here, Anthony was here, and for the moment, Hannah was here.

"Then you have to tell her how you feel." Anthony grabbed his shoulder and shook him. "She'd stay for you, I'm sure of it."

Nicholas wasn't certain. "You didn't hear her talking about it. She wants this."

"Did she say she wanted to leave?"

"She said that Edith's life looked nice." Nicholas ran his hand over his face and tried to ignore the ache in his chest.

"That doesn't mean she wants to leave. There's a lot about Edith's life other than living on Mother Land. What if she wants the companionship Edith and her husband have? You'd be the solution!" Anthony's voice rose to a dangerous volume.

"Will you hush?" Nicholas hissed and checked that the rest of the crew hadn't grown curious about Anthony's outburst. "You're missing the obvious possibility where I tell her how I feel and she leaves because that's too much for her to handle!"

"What if you don't tell her and she leaves because of it?" Anthony's question chilled Nicholas. "Wouldn't it be better to tell her? Have a chance at keeping her than to lose her because you didn't try?"

"Are you saying you'll try if I don't?" The thought had crossed Nicholas's mind before and while the rational part of his brain told him he was crazy, he needed to hear it from Anthony to believe it.

"You're mad if you think that." Anthony shoved him, but Nicholas breathed out in relief. "Hannah is like my little sister. I'm thrilled you feel for her the way you do, but I can't say I could ever see myself in a relationship, especially not with Hannah."

"Thank you." Nicholas finally smiled.

"So you'll tell her?"

"Anthony—"

"At least dance with her. I'll go back to my pipes, and we'll play her favorite song. You'll have an excuse to ask her." He moved away from their spot at the railing before Nicholas could object.

Nicholas wanted to argue, but he didn't dare speak loud enough to stop Anthony's retreat. Anthony turned back to Nicholas and pointed at Hannah.

It was only a dance.

He'd danced with Hannah before and not told her how she swam through his mind like a whale through a school of fish. Certainly he could do it again.

Nicholas steadied himself with a deep breath and walked to Hannah.

"May I cut in?" He tapped David on the shoulder and forced a smile, trying to exude more confidence than he felt.

David released his daughter before she could answer and nodded to Nicholas. "Always my boy." He kissed Hannah on the cheek. "Enjoy yourselves. I've neglected my wife long enough."

Hannah rolled her eyes before sliding into Nicholas's arms and he swore the Sea settled beneath him as he pulled her just a little closer.

"My favorite song and my favorite dance partner. The Sea must think I deserve a treat tonight." Hannah looked up at him, and Nicholas prayed she wouldn't look down at his chest and see his heart beating through his shirt.

"If anyone deserves a treat now and then, it's you." Her small hand fit so well in his, and he pushed away the errant thought of holding her hand off the dance floor. Instead, he focused on how the torchlight flickered up at him in her brown eyes as they moved through the rather formal steps of the dance.

Hannah's face broke out in a soft smile. That look was going to break him if he didn't do something about it.

Nicholas moved them into one of the more lively dances they'd learned while docked at a port, forcing her to look down for a moment and break the hold she had over him. The cool night air flooded his lungs as his ability to breathe returned. "And if anyone deserves to share in that treat, it's me." He finally responded.

"Then I owe you the next dance." She smirked as he spun her out and back into his arms.

"I think you'd owe me two. After all, I helped you with that awful hilt decoration."

Her eyes flashed, and she pulled closer to him. "Then you owe me a dance for keeping a sword out of your head."

He loved the fight in her. She was everything. Everything he wanted. Maybe he could do this, maybe he could tell her he wanted more than the life of friendship they'd enjoyed up to this point.

"What number are we up to?" He asked.

"I've lost count."

Nicholas flinched as Hannah deliberately stepped on his toe and smirked up at him while he tried to keep a straight face. "That's another dance you owe me."

"Then I suppose you'll be stuck dancing with me for the rest of the night." Hannah flipped a stray lock of hair from her face with a laugh.

Nicholas dodged another couple and shifted them into the shadows, away from the rest of the crew as they danced the slower, refined steps of their aristocratic days. "I suppose I will. I accept your offer. We'll dance for the rest of the night and call it even."

"Aye, we'll call it even." Hannah's smile glowed brighter than every torch on the deck.

Dancing the night away with Hannah wrapped in his arms, Nicholas considered Anthony might be right. She might feel the same for him as he felt for her. And if she didn't know how he felt, there was nothing to keep her here. Maybe he did need to make his feelings known, or he'd lose her for good.

All too soon, the music stopped for the evening. Nicholas floundered for words as he let his arms drop from around her, trying to determine what he wanted to say, but Hannah grabbed his wrist and pulled him across the deck.

"I'm not ready to turn in yet. Let's get Anthony and go look at the stars for a while."

Nicholas scoured his mind for a reason that they shouldn't have Anthony join them for stargazing, but his brain had stopped working.

"Anthony!" Hannah reached their friend near the forecastle deck. "Come stargazing with us."

"You two go." He gestured to the waves. "The Sea wanted to talk to me and I asked her to wait till we finished playing. I lose the beat when I talk and play."

Hannah looked up at Nicholas and rolled her eyes. "It's like he's married to her."

Nicholas laughed and pulled Hannah under his arm, his ability to think returning with her teasing. "I don't think that's possible."

"Believe me," Anthony scoffed. "The Sea is not interested in that sort of thing. Or if she is, she has been kind enough not to discuss it with me." He shuddered.

"I wonder if it's even possible to find a woman to marry you." Hannah teased him. "The Sea might swallow up any prospects we brought around."

Anthony gave Nicholas a pointed look and Nicholas could hear the unspoken push to get on with it in his friend's raised brow.

"Leave Anthony to the voice in his head and let's go watch the stars till you're ready for the bunks." He dropped his arm from her shoulders to her waist, nodding to Captain Roberts and Maggie as they passed.

Hannah huffed but waved goodnight to Anthony and his parents and let Nicholas turn her toward the center of the deck.

"Did you want to go to the poop deck?" Nicholas stepped closer to her, breathing in her warm, almost spicy scent.

"I don't want to keep it from Anthony. Let's climb to the crow's nest; we can see everything from there."

"There is not enough room for both of us in the crow's nest." Nicholas countered, but followed her to the mainmast.

"Of course there is. I've been up there with Mother before." Hannah stepped out from under his arm and grabbed the rope ladder.

Nicholas took hold of the other side of the ladder and leaned closer, moving into her space and gaining confidence in how she didn't back away. "You and your mother are the same size. I'm twice your size on my own."

"You are not twice my size." Hannah pushed his shoulder with her free hand, coming close enough for him to count the specks of copper in her brown eyes before the ladder swung her back.

"I am." Nicholas stood to his full height.

"No." Hannah let go of the ladder to step closer to him.

For a moment, Nicholas forgot what they were talking about, and he gripped the rough rope in his hand to stay upright against the force trying to pull him down to Hannah's full, smirking lips.

"This." She set her hand on his chest where her shoulder hit. "Is not half of you."

Nicholas couldn't answer. He couldn't breathe. She stood within a breath of him. His heart beat so loudly there was no way she couldn't hear it. His eyes dropped back to her lips, tracing their curve. Hannah's breath caught, and Nicholas snapped his gaze back to her eyes. Desire looked back at him, and Nicholas leaned forward. She wanted this. He could see it in her eyes. She wanted him. Her hand slipped from his chest to his right bicep and her fingers curled around his sleeve. Her lips parted, but she said nothing. The moonlight illuminated her face in a soft glow, ensnaring him further. He grabbed her waist to steady himself against the swaying ladder, pulling them closer.

"Nicholas?" His name was a breath on her lips.

He froze, realizing that their noses were almost touching. "Aye, Hannah."

"Maybe." She bit her lip. "Maybe we won't fit."

"I'm willing to try if you want to." He swallowed against the gravel in his voice. Her eyes dropped a moment before snapping back to his. He moved in closer, bringing their lips within a breath of each other, praying for her to say yes.

"I—" Her hold on his shirt tightened for a moment. Then her hand pulled away so fast he worried if an oceanfly bit her.

"I only now remembered. I'm on breakfast duty in the morning." She tripped over the words as she stepped back. "I'll...I'll see you tomorrow."

Nicholas blinked, and Hannah disappeared down the steps into the ship. He stood rooted to the deck as his lungs tried to collapse from the ache in his chest. He'd been wrong. He'd read her wrong. Hannah didn't want him as more than a friend.

Hannah wanted off *The Siren*, and there was nothing Nicholas could do to make her stay.

Chapter Three
Hiding Is (Not?) A Solution

Hannah ducked behind a stack of barrels near the steps to the main deck and listened to the heavy tread of footsteps get louder. She held her breath, the smell of barreled grain stuck in her nose, her heart beating in her ears, until finally the footsteps shifted to the wooden slats above her.

Relief flooded Hannah, followed by a tidal wave of guilt.

Hannah had spent the entire day after her terrifying encounter with Nicholas, hiding from him. She knew it frustrated him. His sporadic attempts to find her had increased throughout the day, testing Hannah's ability to think on her feet. She'd been a fair hide and seek player as a child, but after today she had the skills to hide from anything and anyone. Now that twilight had fallen, she determined it safe enough to hide from him above deck, and get some much needed fresh air.

She shouldn't be hiding from him. Nicholas was her best friend. He meant more to her than Mother Land, the Sea and the Sky.

But he wouldn't leave *The Siren*.

As much as Hannah had wanted to give in and kiss him under the stars last night, her dream of a family of her own screamed not to be forgotten. If she gave in and kissed him, she'd never be able to leave *The Siren*. She was already too attached to Nicholas. Kissing him would tie her to this ship for good. But not kissing him might have lost her the chance altogether.

And it killed her.

He'd been right there, all but telling her he wanted more with how his hand had gripped her waist. She could still feel his taut muscle through his shirt sleeve beneath her fingers. Every glimpse of him today stole her breath. Everything she'd ever wanted with him was within her grasp. Everything except children of her own. If she took this dream, she'd be forever shutting the door on another.

Tears pressed against her eyes, and Hannah launched out of her hiding spot for the main deck. She needed the cool evening air to help her regain some control. With a quick glance around the deck from the stairs's shadow, Hannah slipped from the steps into the evening air.

And the sickening heat.

No wonder it had been so unbearable below deck all day. Where she hoped for the cool breeze of night, Hannah found the setting sun had done little to diminish the heat of the day. A windy gale tossed her hair in her face, and Hannah wondered if she'd somehow angered the Sky and this was part of her punishment.

"There you are," Anthony called out.

Hannah froze, wishing she'd been a little more careful to check the deck before emerging from below. In her efforts to avoid Nicholas, she'd inadvertently avoided Anthony, too.

"Aye, here I am." She scanned the deck, praying to Mother Land that Nicholas wasn't anywhere close enough to hear Anthony over the wind.

Anthony rushed to her side, like he feared she would try to run. Rightfully so, as that had been Hannah's first impulse.

"Hannah, why are you avoiding Nicholas and me today?" He adjusted the strip of fabric he'd tied around his forehead. "Are you mad at us?"

Hannah flinched at the hurt in Anthony's voice. "No."

Why hadn't she been more careful? If she had been, she would have seen Anthony and been able to hide again. Now he wouldn't leave her alone until she told him what was wrong, or he pushed her to Nicholas.

"Then what's going on?"

"I'm not avoiding you." Hannah hedged and inched back to the stairs. She might be faster than him. She had been when she was nine and he'd been ten.

"But you are avoiding Nicholas?" Anthony's frown deepened.

The wind threw her hair in her mouth and eyes, trying to knock her off balance on the steps. Hannah spat and wished she'd braided it rather than tied it back as she tried to remain upright. "Come on, I can't think while the wind is trying to blind and gag me. Let's get below."

She turned back down the stairs and led Anthony towards the bow and the empty galley. Plenty of cupboards she could hide in if Nicholas found them.

"I might be avoiding Nicholas." She pushed herself up to sit on the counter, wiping the sweat from her palms on her pants.

"Did something happen last night?" Anthony didn't look at her as he asked, and Hannah rolled her eyes at his attempt to not let on.

"Nicholas already told you what happened last night."

"He told me his side, but you have your own version of what happened." Anthony met her gaze. "I want to know what you think happened last night."

She looked up at the ceiling and let out a long breath. A part of her wanted to tell him; to free herself from the maze of her mind, losing her sanity while replaying the scene over again and again.

Anthony pushed up and sat next to her. "Talk to me."

"I don't even know how it happened. We went to watch the stars. He was teasing me, and then..." she trailed off, watching an oceanfly buzz around the black stove, not sure what to say next.

"Come on." Anthony bumped her shoulder. "You know you can trust me."

She did trust him. Anthony was closer to her than a brother. But she couldn't tell him she wanted to leave. She'd promised to inherit *The Siren* with him when his parents chose to retire. It would crush him if he thought she might leave. Hannah had to keep that part of the story to herself. She'd hurt Anthony enough today.

"Then we almost kissed." The word 'almost' grated on Hannah's heart, but it was better this way. Wasn't it?

"Is that a bad thing?" Anthony wrapped his arm around her shoulders.

"I don't know? It feels like it could be." She picked at a fraying thread on her shirt and sighed. "He's my best friend, Anthony."

"What am I? Shark bait?" Anthony pressed his free hand against his heart in mock offense.

"You're the closest thing I have to an annoying older brother." Hannah shoved him with her shoulder, and Anthony laughed as he lowered his arm.

"I don't see why this is a bad thing." He pulled out a bari stick from his pocket and offered it to her. Hannah shook her head, and Anthony slid it between his teeth. Citrus filled her nostrils as he spoke again. "Can't you tell Nicholas that you aren't positive yet, but you're willing to see where things go?"

Hannah looked down at her boots while she groped for a reason to give Anthony for why she couldn't see where things went with Nicholas. She already knew where she wanted things to go, but she knew they'd never get there. Nicholas would never leave *The Siren*. And Anthony would capsize if he knew she wanted to leave. She'd change the wind of this entire conversation if she told him.

"What if we ruin our friendship by trying to be more?" She kept her eyes on the black leather of her boots, too much of a coward to look Anthony in the eye while she kept her secret from him.

"What if you lose Nicholas because you don't admit to him how you feel?"

Anthony's question cut through her heart as her head snapped up to look at him.

His eyebrows drew together as he continued. "Sometimes things aren't supposed to stay the same. Change is the only constant in life. The Sea taught me that. There are things about us that stay consistent, but most everything else changes, and usually those changes are good ones." Anthony hopped off the counter and turned to face her. "Think about it. If you and Nicholas grow to love each other, you might find a lot of those changes you fear will be good changes."

He pulled the bari stick out of his mouth and smiled at her before walking out of the galley.

Hannah stared after him, his words echoing in her ears.

What if Nicholas changed?

What if knowing she wanted children would change his mind about leaving *The Siren*? What if she could have everything she wanted?

The hope burned in her chest. It was a risk, but it gave her a chance at everything she'd ever dreamed of. She didn't know how they'd work around the fact that the crew could only lose one more person. But if there was any chance she could have a family with Nicholas, she didn't want to lose it. And Anthony's words hinted she could lose Nicholas by not telling him how she felt. Had Nicholas said something to make Anthony worry Nicholas might leave *The Siren*?

Oh, by the Sea, Hannah hoped that was the case.

She hopped off the counter; she needed to decide what to say, and then she needed to talk to Nicholas.

As she walked to the stairs that led down to the bunks, her attention focused on how she might approach Nicholas. Whatever he answered, she'd be able to decide if she'd join Edith or not from it. If he wouldn't leave *The Siren* for her...

Hannah stumbled and caught herself against the wall. That thought almost snuffed out the small fire of hope in her chest. Could she survive him telling her he wouldn't, or couldn't, leave *The Siren* for her?

"Hannah? Hannah, are you all right?" That voice sent her heart racing. She wasn't ready for this conversation. Not yet.

"Aye."

Nicholas came into the light in front of her. "Are you sure? It looked like you fell into the wall."

The sweat on Hannah's face dripped off her cheeks as her heartbeat echoed in her ears.

She must have looked a sight, because Nicholas snatched his water skin from his belt and wrapped an arm around her shoulders.

"Don't pass out on me. Drink."

Hannah took the waterskin, trying to ignore how her body surrendered to his embrace. He smelled of the salt air and sweat, and his arm held her close against his side. Every bone in her body cried out to throw caution to the wind and kiss the man. But Hannah knew her heart would never recover from it. She had to be strong. She brought the waterskin to her mouth and pushed back the ridiculous thought that she could taste him in the water.

"Thanks." She handed him back his waterskin, letting her fingers linger against his a moment longer than she should have. Why, oh why, of all the crew, did he have to be the one to find her?

"Of course. What are friends for?"

Hannah's stomach sank at the word friend. She'd been an awful friend today. And she was in no mental state to make amends for her behavior, let alone tell him what she felt for him. But she owed him something for how she'd treated him today. Hannah met his concerned gaze and fought back the feeling that this could be the last time he held her.

"I want to talk to you. Not now, I'm not ready, but tomorrow. Can we talk tomorrow morning?"

Nicholas nodded, his arm sliding away from her, his fingers tracing her back before falling away. She couldn't breathe.

"Just find me when you're ready." His throat bobbed.

Hannah forced herself to take a step back so she wouldn't walk right back into his embrace. "I will, thank you."

"And Hannah." He caught her hand before she could pull further away. "You can tell me anything."

She bit her lip and nodded, desperate to get to the bunks, to sort through her thoughts, to plan what she wanted to say to him.

"I'll see you tomorrow then." He released her hand and headed back towards the stairs to the main deck.

It wasn't until he stepped out of sight that Hannah's breathing returned to normal. Hannah headed to her bed, resigned to the fact that she'd spend most of the night staring at the slats above her bunk while her mind sped through her thoughts like a ship at full sail in a storm.

CHAPTER FOUR
Drowning

Nicholas rested his arms on the railing, looking out at the Sea. The sun sat low on the morning horizon, but sweat already dripped down his back. He hated these heat spells that overpowered even the wind that should have cooled him. They pushed a sailor into cabin fever at the worst, and surly at best. Nicholas sat somewhere between the two at the moment, but he couldn't blame all of his bad mood on the heat.

He was an idiot, plain and simple.

Hannah had made that clear by not only avoiding him but actively hiding from him the whole day yesterday. And the way she told him she wanted to talk to him at some point today increased his certainty that he had not only lost their friendship, but had pushed her to pursue a way to leave *The Siren*.

Why hadn't he kept his mouth shut? He'd kept his feelings for her to himself for a decade, and now he ruined it by opening his fat mouth. Every now and again, Nicholas found something his fifteen-year-old self understood better than he did now, and each time he did, it grated on him.

She'd spoken to Anthony, but Anthony wasn't saying anything. Nicholas had always appreciated Anthony's ability to keep things to himself, but right now Nicholas needed something, anything, to throw him a rescue rope. His mind had fallen overboard, drowning in his anxiety while he waited for Hannah to show up and sink his heart to the ocean floor.

It was going to kill him when she left. Hannah infused every part of this ship. Her ghost would haunt him from the wood slats for the rest of his life. She'd always be standing next to him at the rigging or laying on the poop deck looking at the stars anytime he went there to think. He hadn't realized it till yesterday, but his world revolved around her. *The Siren* might be where he lived, but Nicholas's sleepless night proved to him that Hannah made it his home. When she left, she'd drive him mad and she wouldn't be anywhere near him.

Maybe he should leave too.

The guilt that followed that errant thought kicked him in the chest and left a sour taste in his mouth. The old crew members depended on *The Siren* sailing to keep them and their new families safe. He couldn't leave, especially if Hannah did. But staying might drive him mad, and what good would he be to *The Siren's* crew then? Perhaps he'd leave and attempt to assassinate Corny Jr. That way, Hannah could tell whatever landsman she married her real name.

Nicholas leaned further over the railing as his heart gave out for a terrifying moment. He couldn't stay on *The Siren*. It would kill him to go into port and see her with someone else. Cabin fever would be tame compared to the insanity he'd face. If Hannah left, he'd have to leave. There had to be a way for two more crew members to leave. He'd talk to the Merfolk, figure something out. Marious was the merman that found them; perhaps he would understand, and if he didn't, his son, Mahindra, was a good friend. He might have an idea. If they couldn't help him, Nicholas would intercede with Anthony, and to the Sea herself. Somehow, he'd get off this ship.

He had to.

The ship heaved, throwing Nicholas from the railing and onto his shoulder, before slamming back into the Sea. Nicholas stumbled to his feet with the rest of the crew that had toppled to the deck.

"Anthony!" Captain Roberts emerged from his quarters.

"Captain!" Anthony leaned over the poop deck railing, his grip on it turning his knuckles white.

"Report!"

"I don't know. I've asked the Sea, but she isn't answering me."

Captain Roberts frowned and moved to the starboard railing where the ship had tipped and the crew slowly gathered. Nicholas joined them, looking down into the deep blue water. He couldn't see anything unusual. There were a few creatures swimming around. He caught sight of a pair of Speckled Chirper Fish gliding beneath the surface, and while they were big enough for a man to sit on their back, they were nowhere big enough to rock *The Siren*.

"She sneezed?" Anthony quipped as he came to stand next to them.

Nervous laughter rippled through the crew but didn't lighten anyone's mood as more came up from below deck.

"Has she said anything to you yet?" Captain Roberts spoke low to Anthony. "I don't like how far we shifted. We're a hundred feet away from where we were."

Nicholas shifted closer to hear Anthony's response. Only the biggest monsters of the Sea moved ships that far. As much as Nicholas wanted off *The Siren* when Hannah left, he didn't want to be off her in the middle of open water. They were days away from any shore.

Anthony shook his head. "I'll pester her. Sometimes I have to be persistent to get her to answer."

Nicholas grabbed Anthony's arm before he could run back to the poop deck.

"How far are we from the Mer Sea?"

"About three hours at full sail, but it's not the same part of the Mer Sea where our island is."

Nicholas kept his voice low. "Could something from there have ventured out to these waters?"

The sea monsters's home was the Mer Sea where the Merfolk kept all ships but *The Siren* out. While it wasn't unheard of for a monster to venture into trafficked waters, it wasn't common.

"Maybe." Anthony frowned. "I'll ask her that instead. It might be a better question than what I've been asking." He moved back to the poop deck with the blank stare that always accompanied him speaking to the Sea.

Nicholas hoped the Sea thought his question better than whatever Anthony asked the first time. Knowing the Sea cared about how Anthony asked things confused him almost as much as what tipped the ship.

"Nicholas?"

"Hannah." Nicholas took a deep breath against the ache in his chest and turned to face her. She'd braided her hair in two long braids down her back, tying a strap of deep red fabric around her forehead to combat this oppressive heatwave. The red pulled the copper out of her brown eyes, eyes that looked at him with trepidation. It took as much strength to pull the rigging as it took to not pull her into him and beg her to not break his heart just yet.

"Do you," she stopped and cleared her throat. "Do you know what rocked the ship?"

A part of him was glad the ship rocking pushed her to postpone that conversation she wanted to have. But a larger part wanted her to sink him and be done with it.

"No. Anthony's trying to get the Sea to tell him what happened. None of us saw it."

Hannah nodded and glanced up at the poop deck before looking down at her boots. "I wanted to talk to you about—"

The ship surged, slamming against the calm waters and knocking them off their feet. Instinct took over and Nicholas pulled Hannah to him, keeping her above him as they hit the deck. Every part of her pressed against his body as she curled into his embrace.

What he wouldn't give to keep her there.

"Anthony!" Captain Roberts shouted.

"She's not answering!" Anthony called back.

"Yell louder, my boy!"

The ship tipped again, sending Nicholas and Hannah and the rest of the crew rolling across the deck. Hannah gripped his shirt and wrapped one leg around his as the two spiraled over the planks. He tightened his hold on her, trying to keep his full weight from crushing her beneath him. His shoulder hit the railing with a whack that Nicholas knew would bruise, but he didn't dare release Hannah. When she told him she was through with him, this would be all he had left. These stolen moments of holding her in his arms, pretending she could have been his.

A loud bellow sounded below them, and Hannah gasped as Nicholas's heart sank.

"Sea serpent!" Captain Roberts roared.

The captain's whistle called out orders, and Nicholas forced himself to loosen his hold on Hannah. Instead of jumping up, as he expected, she buried her head in the crook of his neck. He pulled her close again and breathed her in, thanking the Sea, Sky and Mother Land that she was giving him one more moment like this.

"Don't die." She murmured against his neck. Then she pushed up and ran for the rigging.

Nicholas couldn't watch her go and he pushed away the hope that maybe she wouldn't sink him when they got a second chance at this conversation. He'd have feelings for that later. Now, he ran for the muskets.

He hated sea serpents. Ships didn't fight sea serpents. A crew couldn't defeat something ten times the length of their ship and as wide as two. Thankfully, the Sea had the foresight to make sea serpents a bit slower than a ship at full sail. With a good wind a ship could outrun the monster, and her crew could deter it with musket fire until they were ahead of it. That was assuming the sea serpent didn't capsize the ship before the crew caught the wind and made good their escape.

Nicholas took his place along the port side railing at the base of the quarterdeck stairs, watching for any sign of the monster through the hazy heat. *The Siren* lurched forward as those assigned to the rigging unfurled the sails. He turned and caught sight of Hannah helping with the ropes; her face set as she held fast to the rigging.

The ship healed back; the poop deck tipping toward the water. Nicholas tore his eyes from Hannah and clung to the railing as the ship's bow slammed back against the waves.

Sea, Sky and Mother Land help them.

"Anthony!" Nicholas yelled along with several of the crew. He ran up the quarterdeck stairs, stopping just shy of the deck when Anthony came into view, leaning over the poop deck railing.

"I'm fine!" He waved Nicholas off and looked at his parents standing near the helm. "The Sea is answering! She's going to push us away!"

An enormous shadow eclipsed the sun, and Nicholas's hair stood on end. He welcomed the relief from the heat, but dread filled him as he looked up from the stairs. A blue green head the size of *The Siren*, spiked fins coming from its head as tall as the mainmast, loomed above him. The serpent transfixed Nicholas. Its fangs protruding from its mouth were longer than Nicholas was tall, and beyond them a black hole led into the sea serpent's gullet.

The sound of musket fire brought him out of his daze, and Nicholas shook himself. The crew didn't need him admiring the snake the way he admired Hannah. If he kept that up, he'd be a dead man. Any hope of a life with Hannah would sink with him. He pulled his musket to his shoulder, aiming for the sea serpent's eye, and fired.

The monster's head flinched back under the barrage of musket balls. Nicholas mused it must feel the way he did when flies flew in his face. The snake whipped back with speed Nicholas didn't believe the beast could possess, and snapped at the ship. Nicholas's instincts pushed him forward, reaching for the railing. If the snake rammed the ship and threw him backward this far up the stairs, his crash to the deck would break something.

For not the first time this week, Nicholas was wrong.

The sea serpent didn't ram *The Siren*. Its snap had been a warning.

Nicholas swore as he failed to stop his forward momentum. This was not what he meant when he wished to be off *The Siren*. He fell headfirst over the railing, his sweaty fingers slipping away from the wood, and he smacked against the scaled back of the sea serpent. Instinct kicked in again, this time choosing to be useful as Nicholas pulled his boot knife and stabbed it into the sea serpent's scales, ensuring he wouldn't find himself under this monster. The snake arched and dove into the water. Nicholas looked up one more time at *The Siren*, moving at top speed away from him. Water filled his vision, fighting to fill his lungs.

And to think he'd been worried about Hannah sinking him. If only he'd known a sea serpent would steal the opportunity out from under her.

CHAPTER FIVE
When Emotion And Logic Collide

"Nicholas!"

The call for man-overboard blared again and again as Hannah ran from the rigging to the port railing. She hit the wood and her whistle popped out of her mouth to hang from its cord, cutting off the call. The sea serpent's coils rolled beneath the surface, blending into the depths of the water. Hannah's eyes darted from coil to coil, desperate for any sign of the man she'd finally worked up the courage to tell how she felt.

"Hannah, watch out!" Anthony's yell pulled her back as the ship heaved again, the sea serpent's body knocking them around like driftwood in the waves. She dropped and clung to the railing as the ship yawed, but didn't capsize.

She scanned the Sea and held her breath in panic that the entire crew might soon join Nicholas in the waves.

"I see him!" Anthony shouted.

Hannah caught Anthony's eye as the ship righted itself. He pointed toward *The Siren's* bow, and when she turned, she caught sight of Nicholas, clinging to his boot dagger lodged in the snake's back.

Nicholas!

The sea serpent's head shot from the water closer to the ship than before. *The Siren* tilted as Maggie spun the helm, turning them away from the monster and Nicholas. Hannah didn't think. She pulled her dagger from her boot, then launched herself upward, jumping from the railing and off *The Siren*. She braced as she fell onto the sea serpent, slamming her dagger into the snake's neck.

The sea serpent bellowed and reared back, almost dislodging her dagger. Hannah recoiled at the scales articulating beneath her. Her stomach heaved at the snake's stench. The monster smelled of rot and the sound of its scales scratching against each other set her teeth on edge. But she had to get to Nicholas.

Hannah turned to look for him when her vision filled with the Sea.

She didn't stop her instinct to gasp, bringing water into her lungs.

No, no, no!

This wasn't what was supposed to happen today.

Let it surface! She begged all Three Sisters.

One must have heard her. Hannah came up out of the Sea and let her lungs cough. Three heartbeats and then the snake dove back into the frigid waves. That was the pattern. Three heartbeats to cough up as much water from her lungs as she could before the snake would take her under again, holding her there till her lungs burned. Panic set in after the sea serpent dove for the millionth time. The colors were muting around her.

The snake would not surface again.

Her neck cracked as she whipped around for any sign of Nicholas. Nothing. Hannah couldn't wait any longer. If she didn't let go now, the monster would take her too deep to surface before she drowned. Praying Nicholas had already surfaced, Hannah set her feet on the snake's awful scales and launched herself toward the light above her.

Her lungs burned to cough as Hannah kicked with all her strength. This was not how she wanted to die. She wanted to die old in her bed, surrounded by those she loved. Not drowning somewhere south of the Mer Sea when *The Siren* was close enough to save her. The hope pushed her on, giving her an extra burst to propel herself upward.

Hannah refused to die so close to her rescue.

Light blinded her as she finally broke through the surface and allowed her lungs to expel the water in them. It wasn't until her lungs took in a full breath that Hannah looked around her and her blood turned colder than the water she was treading.

The Siren was gone.

In a frantic spin, she scanned the waves, hoping for any sign of her home.

Nothing.

Water for leagues with no sign of ships or land.

Adrift.

Hannah sputtered as a wave hit her in the face.

She was adrift. The sea serpent must have taken her in a different direction than *The Siren*, whose sails were moving it at full sail away from the snake.

Sails she'd helped unfurl.

No. No. No.

They'd never find her.

Hannah had no power against the waves as they pushed her through the Sea. *The Siren* was leagues away from her by now. This was the end. She couldn't tread water forever, and when her body gave out, she would slip below the waves, joining all the Nerland sailors she'd killed in their watery grave.

And to think she thought the hardest part of her day would be the possibility of Nicholas rejecting her.

Hannah squeezed her eyes against the tears. Should she end it? If there was no reason to fight, why die frozen and exhausted? It could be over now, while she still had some warmth, while her mind was still whole.

A loud chirp sounded and Hannah screamed as a Speckled Chirper Fish pushed up to the surface below her. Its white skin speckled with yellow and blue reflecting the sun back into her eyes. She gripped its smooth fin with one hand and shielded her eyes with the other.

Of course, something would save her just when she was thinking of ending it all.

"There's no use rescuing me." She tucked her legs against her chest, helping to block the light reflecting into her eyes. "My ship is long gone."

The term fish didn't serve these creatures. It turned its head around to look at her with its massive, round eyes. A strange cross between a shell-less turtle, a seal, and a squid, Hannah was of the opinion that whoever called them fish must have been drunk when they named it. The Merfolk called them Cuddlers, as they mated for life and, once mated, spent most of their life swimming side by side.

Hannah frowned, realizing that this Cuddler was alone.

"Where's your mate?" She looked around as the fish chirped at her in what sounded an awful lot like talking.

She should have drowned herself when she had the chance. She was going mad already.

Hannah swallowed her scream as something large and dark several yards off started moving towards them. She definitely should have drowned herself when she had the chance. Now she was going to be ripped apart by whatever monster had tracked her scent.

"Hurry! If you leave me here, it'll eat me and you'll have time to get away." She pushed off the Cuddler, but it gave a sharp chirp before its fin smacked her back.

"I'm going to die, anyway! No sense in both of us getting eaten!" She pushed against its fin, but the fish smacked her harder this time, chirping angrily.

Hannah looked back at the monster gaining on them, trying to determine what creature was about to tear her apart and have her for lunch. The more she focused on it, though, the more it looked like the torso of a man.

So this was what sea madness did to a woman, seeing men in monsters.

It wasn't until the monster came closer that Hannah realized what swam toward her.

Nicholas's body draped over the back of another Cuddler.

Unmoving.

"Nicholas!"

Her fish must have sensed her distress, for it moved to meet the fish carrying Nicholas.

"Please don't be dead." If he was dead, she wouldn't hesitate to drown herself.

Hannah grabbed hold of Nicholas's shirt and pulled him to her chest. Her fingers found his neck, and she held her breath as she prayed for a pulse.

His heart beat faintly against her fingertips.

"Thank Mother Land!" Hannah wanted to cry, but she pushed the tears aside to focus. While there was a pulse, it wasn't as strong as it should be, and his breathing was shallow. She didn't have any way to call on Mother Land's healing with fire and color. Saving Nicholas would require sailor's healing. She pushed up to her knees and grunted as she pulled him further onto her fish, turning him to his left side. What she wouldn't give for a ship's deck. His torso needed to be above his head, but as Hannah tried to adjust Nicholas over her knees, water splashed into his face.

She yanked him back up and glared at the fish. "Can you lift us any further out of the water?"

The Cuddlers both looked up at her and she swore they wore exasperated expressions. She was going mad. Hannah shifted again, doing her best to keep Nicholas's face out of the water as she gave his ribs staccato taps.

"Come on, Nicholas, you've got to breathe the water out."

She focused on her tapping, watching his chest rise and fall. If he were awake, she'd tell him to breathe from his stomach. If he were awake, they wouldn't be doing this because he would have made it up to the surface before he half drowned.

If he were awake, she wouldn't have to die alone.

That thought brought her up short. A few moments ago, she considered drowning herself. But here she sat, doing everything in her power to bring Nicholas back. For what? So they could die together?

Yes. A selfish voice sounded within her. That was exactly why. She didn't want to die alone. If she could wake him, they could die together.

Because that was somehow better than dying alone.

And maybe she could still tell him of her feelings, like she'd planned to do this morning.

An age later, Nicholas coughed and Hannah forced herself not to speed up her tapping. Coughing meant this was working. Eons passed and worlds fell out of existence while Nicholas coughed. Hannah's hand ached from the strain of keeping her tapping steady and not giving into the desire to pound on his ribs as fast as she could. The chill from the water wore off, replaced with the beating sun and kiln warmed breeze. Hannah wiped the sweat from her brow on her shoulder and prayed Nicholas would gain consciousness before her arm fell off.

"Enough." Nicholas coughed harder. "Enough. Let me up."

"Not yet." Hannah's body ached with the effort to stay calm. "Deep breaths, from your stomach, not your shoulders."

She watched his chest and belly expand fully, and Nicholas coughed harder as he exhaled.

Music to her ears.

"That's it, keep going."

"Sea and Sky, this hurts."

"Focus on breathing."

He stopped talking. Breathing in full breaths and coughing out water on his exhales till his breathing sounded normal and his pulse was almost as strong as her own.

"All right, let me up." Nicholas pushed against the Cuddlers beneath them, shifting so he was sitting on the one that had rescued him.

Hannah flinched as she watched the light in his eyes go dull. From the position she'd had him in, he couldn't see their reality. But now...

"Adrift." The word slipped from him, as if he couldn't believe it. "I..." he trailed off.

The sound of the ocean filled the space between them as Nicholas looked around at the open water. He dropped his head to his chest and slackened his grip on his pants. Hannah couldn't bear to watch the hopelessness fill him. Who knew the view of nothing but the Sea could go from comforting to agonizing over the course of a few hours?

"Are you mad that I got you breathing again?" She asked, worried he knew her selfish motives behind saving him.

Nicholas sighed, his shoulders sagging as he shook his head. "I'm glad my last memory before I die won't be that Sky awful snake."

Relief filled her.

"But," he continued, and Hannah's relief halted. "How in Mother Land's name did you end up here? You were at the rigging when I fell overboard."

Her face heated, even with the cold water still dripping from her hair. He would not like her answer, and somewhere in the morning's chaos, she used up the courage she summoned to tell him of her feelings for him. Now embarrassment burned in her stomach like she was thirteen again, caught doing something she knew better than to do.

"Hannah?"

She looked down at the yellow and blue speckles on the Cuddlers, not willing to meet his gaze as she admitted to her failure. "I tried to save you."

"How?" Nicholas reached for her, but stopped as his weight shifted and he almost fell into the water.

A stroke of clarity hit Hannah as she scoured her brain for how to articulate her emotions after seeing him clinging to the sea serpent. They were going to die. It was imminent. They had five days left if they were unlucky. Less if the Three Sisters had compassion for them. There would be no taking Edith up on her offer if Nicholas rejected her. She had no future, no chance at a life with children of her own. She had nothing to lose; the sea serpent had taken everything from her.

Everything except Nicholas.

She refused to squander what little time they had left. She'd lost everything except this one chance, and Hannah refused to let fear steal it from her now. "I jumped on the sea serpent to get to you."

"What?"

She expected his voice to be livid, full of anger and at a volume the fish in the Sea's depths would hear him. But the reality proved worse. Nicholas's question came in a quiet, defeated tone, a tone Hannah wished had never come from his lips.

"I thought I could get to you." She echoed his tone and volume. "And get us back to the ship."

Nicholas hung his head, running his hands through his hair and then clasping them behind his neck. "I'm sorry. If I hadn't misjudged the snake, I wouldn't have fallen overboard. We're here because of my mistake."

"No!" Hannah reached for him, losing her balance and grabbing his arm to keep from toppling off her fish. "You couldn't control that the sea serpent found us, or that *The Siren* gained full speed after the two of us were overboard. This isn't your fault."

Nicholas shifted and pulled their fish closer together. Hannah watched the two fish nuzzle their heads, finding the rise of jealousy in her chest ridiculous. She had nothing to be jealous of. Nicholas was here and she wouldn't die alone and she could thank the Three Sisters for it.

"Come here." Nicholas pulled on her hand. "I think the Cuddlers can keep us both up and we need to stretch out." He pushed his legs out in front of him, taking up part of the flat back of her fish.

Hannah shifted and collapsed into Nicholas's embrace as all the emotion and strain of their situation hit her harder than her landing on the sea serpent. "I can't believe we're going to die here."

"Maybe we won't." Nicholas squeezed her shoulders. "Anthony and the Sea might be able to work together to find us. And if not that, there's the possibility that another ship could come this way. Or maybe the Cuddlers will decide to swim toward land."

Hannah shook her head at the strain in his voice. "You don't believe that. We don't have the time for any of it, except maybe Anthony and the Sea."

"I know, but I'm trying to believe it." He sighed. "You're right, though. This is probably where we move on to whatever's next."

Hannah sniffed against the tears that climbed up her throat, pushing them away. She wanted more than tears from her last few days. She wanted Nicholas.

Now she just needed to drudge up the courage to ask.

"I know it must seem mad that I remember this, but," Nicholas paused and took a long breath. "What were you going to talk to me about this morning?"

Apparently, one or more of the Three Sisters wanted her to find that courage.

Hannah leaned further into Nicholas's side. Her damp clothes and boots chafed against her skin and she could feel strands escaping from her braids plastered to her face. Why couldn't they have managed this conversation before the sea serpent attacked? When she didn't look like she'd been drug across the ocean floor and she couldn't smell herself.

"Hannah?"

One cuddler looked back at her and Hannah swore it was trying not to laugh. Her appearance be hanged. She refused to be a coward for these Cuddlers to laugh at. "I wanted to talk to you about how I thought that maybe—if we'd not found ourselves on death's doorstep—we could have been good together."

Nicholas went still. "We are good together."

The caution in his voice almost persuaded her to let it go, to settle for hiding her feelings like she had for years. But the thought of being laughed at by the Cuddlers long after she died chaffed worse than her clothes.

"I thought we could be more. I was going to ask if you wanted more." Hannah looked down at her hands and twisted them in her soaking pant legs. "Like I wanted more."

"Wanted or want?"

"We're going to die. Everything is past tense now."

"Hannah." His hand caressed her chin and Hannah closed her eyes as he guided her face back to him. "Wanted or want?"

"It doesn't matter now." She whispered and scrunched her eyes tighter against the tears trying to push through. "I'm going to lose you."

"You haven't lost me, you can't lose me."

His forehead rested against hers, and Hannah's heart skipped at his promise. Their noses slid together, pulling them closer, mingling their breaths. Or what little breath she had left as she drowned in him. Hannah tried to push the cacophony in her mind away, to focus on the feeling of Nicholas pressed against her, closer than he'd ever been. She didn't know what was next, but she wanted him by her side, even if he didn't want more.

"Want." Hannah tangled her hands in his damp shirt. "I wanted more and I want more."

"I want more too." His low voice rolled through her like the incoming tide. "I wanted more and I want more."

For the second time that day, Hannah didn't think. She pressed forward, bringing her lips to his in the kiss she'd spent years imagining as she stared at the slats above her bunk.

Except it was so much more than she'd dreamed.

Nicholas shifted closer, his arm sliding from her shoulders to wrap around her back, pulling her into him. She gasped when his other hand tangled in her fraying braids, shifting the angle of the kiss, parting her lips and allowing him to slide his tongue against hers. He kissed her like she was all the air left in the world, and Hannah wanted to give her last breath to him.

A quiet part of her laughed, realizing that given their circumstances, she might have that chance.

Chapter Six
Losing Layers

The end of his life wasn't something Nicholas expected to be an enjoyable experience, but he'd imagined it being more comfortable than his current circumstances. His back and shoulders ached from having to sit on their Speckled Chirper raft. His lungs still burned from the water he'd aspirated and, with Hannah's pounding on his lungs, expelled. The cold amplified every other discomfort. Their clothes had mostly dried earlier, but as the sun hung low on the horizon, they'd hit rough waters. Waves soaked them again, and while he was glad for the chance to have Hannah pulled close against him, Nicholas wished they could forego the shivering.

"Yesterday I complained that the heat was unbearable and now I'm going to freeze to death." Hannah snuggled closer to him.

"I suppose it's better than drowning." Nicholas shifted to bring her shaking body against him, his muscles crying out in pain.

She slipped her hand up from his soaked shirt to his neck and he leaned into the warmth it brought.

"Your skin is still a little warm." Hannah hummed as she pushed his shirt further aside and brought her face to rest against his bare skin. The slightest blossom of warmth spread from her cheek across his neck.

"So is yours." The warmth of her skin cleared his mind enough to remember there were methods for keeping warm when the regular options were out of reach.

Options that required less clothing.

That left him slightly embarrassed. Hannah was still his childhood friend. Even if he wanted more, even if he had imagined more in the past, even with them confessing that more was what they both wanted. He pushed the embarrassment to the back of his mind. He didn't want to die shivering in the dark if he could help it. And he had no intention of letting Hannah die in his arms tonight, not when they could have at least one more day together. So he summoned his courage and kept the idea of more at the forefront of his mind.

"Don't take this the wrong way. But I'm going to take my shirt off."

"What?" Hannah shot up, slipping towards the water before Nicholas pulled her back to him.

Their fish chirped sharply at the commotion, looking back at them with what Nicholas could only describe as a reprimand.

"She didn't mean to do it. Relax." He steadied Hannah and glared at their living raft.

The Cuddlers looked at each other, and Nicholas swore the moonlight cast exasperation in their glance. Wonderful. Sea madness was already setting in. He shot the fish another glare. Sea madness or no, he wouldn't let the Cuddlers get after Hannah. The two fish rolled their eyes before turning away. Satisfied, Nicholas turned back to Hannah.

"Our skin is warmer than our clothes for the moment, so I'm going to take off my shirt and keep you from freezing tonight." Nicholas's face grew warmer as he spoke. It wasn't as though he'd never been around a woman with his shirt off. The issue was he'd never been topless while *Hannah* was lying against his chest. "You can keep your shirt on." He hurried to add, not wanting to pressure her. "But I'm going to take mine off."

The moonlight didn't hide the bright red color covering Hannah's cheeks, and Nicholas wasn't sure if he was relieved or not that she shared in his nervous energy. He looked away and ignored how his body screamed against the effort of pulling his shirt over his head. The night air pricked at his skin and his teeth chattered at the sudden drop in temperature. Was it possible to shiver so violently a man could lose all his teeth?

Nicholas shook the thought away and tied his shirt around his waist. With one more deep breath, he turned to look at Hannah.

Who immediately turned away from him.

Maybe this wasn't such a good idea.

"Here." She shifted to sit on the other fish with her back to him. "Don't take this the wrong way." She glanced back, moonlight illuminating the way she pulled her bottom lip between her teeth. "If I try to turn around, I'll slip off again."

To his astonishment, and frankly his pleasure, Hannah pulled her shirt over her head.

Nevermind, this was a good idea.

Nicholas gripped his pant knees, unable to look away. Her back shone silver under the moon's glow. The elegant curve that ran from her neck, beneath the band that held her breasts, then down to her belt mesmerized him more than the Sea Serpent had that morning.

Hannah folded her shirt into a long strip before wrapping it around her breast band and tying it off behind her in a fashion he'd seen at a port they frequented. Nicholas swallowed hard. He hadn't counted on the warmth hitting him before he'd even touched her.

Then Hannah scooted back to his side.

He shouldn't be nervous. This was Hannah. His best friend. The woman who only hours ago told him she wanted more than friendship with him. The woman he had more than once imagined having in situations reminiscent of this one.

That thought got him moving. Nicholas gave into the hunger for the warmth of her body and the feel of her skin beneath his fingers. He shifted her from his side to his front; her back pressed against his chest as his arms held her close. His dreams, his imagination, had nothing on the reality of holding Hannah against his bare chest.

Perhaps he had died, and all of this was a strange afterlife.

"Thank the Sea, you were right." Hannah moaned and let her head fall back against his shoulder, her shaking lessening a small bit. "This is warmer."

Nicholas took advantage of her exposed neck and kissed her skin, wishing they had more time than these few days adrift. "Good. If we can help it, I don't want us dying tonight."

"Having experienced a taste of it, shivering to death is no longer my first choice for execution." Hannah chuckled and burrowed further into his embrace.

"Do you have a new first choice?" Nicholas smiled and held her tighter, feeling warmer for more than one reason.

"If I can get my teeth to stop chattering, it's death by kissing you, but I think we'd bite our tongues out if we attempted it right now."

Nicholas laughed and kissed her temple. "We'll wait till we're warmer then, but if it's all the same to you, I'd rather the kissing not end in our deaths."

"I guess I could pass on the dying and enjoy the kissing." Hannah turned to smile up at him.

For the briefest moment, Nicholas considered if they were warm enough to get on to kissing. Then his chattering teeth bit the inside of his cheek.

Definitely not.

Chapter Seven
Take What You Can Get

Hannah snuggled further into Nicholas's arms, listening to the water slosh around them. They'd been cuddled together long enough now that her teeth had finally stopped chattering like a pod of dolphins sharing gossip. Nicholas's suggestion to remove his shirt had brought out a shyness that Hannah didn't know she possessed. But the shyness evaporated more and more with each passing moment, leaving Hannah wishing for things that weren't an option adrift in open water.

"Do you think the Sea sent us these Cuddlers?" She asked, directing her thoughts away from things that would land them both back in the Sea.

Nicholas chuckled, the sound vibrating against her back and his breath warming her neck. "I want to. They certainly showed up at the right time. I even saw a pair of Cuddlers before the sea serpent attacked. Maybe it was these two."

Hannah let her head rest back against his shoulder and sighed. "It's hard to not think that she sent them because she knows *The Siren* can't get to us."

Nicholas didn't answer her for a long moment.

He sighed and tightened his arms around her. "Aye, you might be right. I'm sorry, Hannah, I wanted so much more for us than this."

"It's not your fault." Hannah swiped away an escaping tear. She had wanted more for them, too. "At least we're together."

His hand cupped her face, tilting her lips up to meet his in a slow kiss. "Aye."

Hannah grabbed the back of his neck and pulled him down to her again, ignoring their chapped lips and the taste of salt. If only this wasn't all they had left. She wanted to ask him all the questions she hadn't had the time to ask. To tell him all the things that she never had the chance to. To tell him how badly she'd wanted to have a family with him. She pulled away, deciding to try to share everything before it was too late.

"Do you believe what the witches say?" Nicholas spoke before she could, his eyes locking on hers with a determination she hadn't seen outside of the battles they'd fought on *The Siren*. "That when we die, our souls ascend into the Sky?"

Hope burned anew in her chest. Maybe she didn't need to tell him everything before they died. "I want to."

Nicholas smiled and pressed his lips back to hers. "I refuse to believe this is the end. When we die, believe the witches, and be with me in the Sky."

"Even if the Witches are wrong, I'll be with you in whatever comes next. If our souls sink to the bottom of the Sea, I'll be with you there." Hannah tightened her fingers around the back of his neck, choosing to believe there was something after this life, something more for them. That she didn't need to share everything with him now. She could tell him about the dreams that would die with her in whatever eternity waited for them.

"I'll find you." Nicholas slid his nose against hers. "I'll be with you in whatever comes next. Forever."

Hannah pressed forward, closing the space between them and kissing Nicholas with a new passion. She'd lost every other dream, lost any hope of children of her own, but she could have this one last thing. She would have Nicholas, and that would have to be enough.

Chapter Eight
Roll The Dice

As much as Nicholas would have preferred it, kissing each other the entire night wasn't an option. But a full night's sleep wasn't in the stars for them either. Every time he dozed off, his body shifted and Nicholas woke with a panicked start. He couldn't afford to fall into the water, or worse, pull Hannah in with him. At a certain point, the cold was enough that they donned their mostly dry shirts again with the hope of more warmth. It helped, but they still shivered through the night. The hours passed in excruciating seconds, leaving Nicholas more exhausted than he'd ever experienced before. By the time the sun's rays broke over the horizon, he privately admitted that drowning themselves after they'd committed to whatever afterlife awaited them might have been the better option.

"How long before you think we'll warm up?" Hannah rubbed her hands up and down her legs.

"A few hours at least." A small black spot on the horizon caught his eye. The dehydration was getting to him. Nicholas rubbed his eyes and tried to ignore it. "Come noon, we'll wish for the night again."

"You wish for night. I'll wish for clean water." Hannah rested her head on his shoulder. Nicholas wrapped her under his arm and chuckled.

That black spot caught his attention again, and he forced his eyes away from it. He intended to push off the insanity for as long as possible.

But as far as insanity went, seeing black spots on the horizon wasn't a terrible way to go about it. He'd heard of sailors hearing voices that weren't there, tormenting them until they surrendered to the madness and gave up the ghost. Black spots on the horizon were a blessing in comparison.

"I'm already getting sea madness." Hannah sighed. "I'm seeing spots on the horizon."

Nicholas froze. Slowly, he looked back to where he'd seen the black spot. It was still right where he'd seen it before. Was it bigger?

"Where did you see the spot?" He kept his hope from his voice.

"It was over..." Hannah trailed off as she looked at the spot on the horizon.

"I see it." He held her close. "If we both see it, we aren't mad yet."

"What if it's not a ship?" She breathed.

"It might not be. Mother Land, it might not even be coming this way. But we can both see it. It's real. And there's a chance whatever it is could get us out of here." Nicholas gripped her shoulders, trying not to let his hopes rise too high on the waves. "Think of it, a chance to live."

"Together." Hannah turned her smile to him, warming his soul.

"Together." He kissed her hair, keeping his eyes on what might be their rescue on the horizon.

They sat quietly, watching the black dot grow as the sun rose higher into the sky. Nicholas went from cold to warm when the black spot grew to the size of an oceanfly. Warm turned to hot about the same time the spot developed some shape to it. When the heat became unbearable, Nicholas knew what the approaching silhouette was.

"Do you think it's *The Siren*?" Hannah gripped his hand tighter than an octopus held onto its dinner.

Nicholas wanted it to be. He wanted it to be *The Siren* more than he wanted anything. Except for how much he wanted a life with Hannah. And a cold drink of water. And something to eat. But all his hopes would be realized if the approaching ship was *The Siren*.

"We can't tell yet." He reigned in his hope. "They can't even see us."

"I want it to be." Hannah kept her eyes focused on the approaching ship as she spoke. "But even if it isn't, I want them to find us. I want a life with you."

"What if they're Nerlanders that recognize us, or worse, pirates?" Nicholas hedged, not sure he wanted to live through what either of those options would mean. "We'd be better off dead than picked up by either of them."

Hannah chuckled, but there was no humor in it. "Then we jump overboard and drown ourselves. But we might have a chance, and I don't want to lose it."

Nicholas shifted to bring her back under his arm. He wanted that chance too; with every fiber of his being, he wanted a life with Hannah wherever he could have it.

He looked at their Speckled Chirpers. "You heard her. If we get picked up by this ship and then jump back off, don't you two come save us a second time."

Hannah laughed, a full laugh that filled Nicholas from the bottom of his soaked boots to the top of his windswept hair. He brought his chapped lips to hers, filling himself with the peace that only Hannah could give him. Whatever happened next, he knew it would be with Hannah by his side. He couldn't ask for anything more than that.

Chapter Nine
Living, Maybe

*T*he *Siren* had truly earned her fearsome reputation. Even as Hannah's heart soared at seeing it approach, a part of her wanted to cower and hide from the ship that sailed toward them.

"It's *The Siren*, right?" Nicholas rubbed his eyes. "I'm not imagining it?"

"It is. It's them." She couldn't believe it. After the sun had shifted toward the western horizon and the ship's course looked to be following it, Hannah forced herself to accept the ship wasn't *The Siren*; and that it would end up too far away to see her and Nicholas, let alone save them.

But the ship corrected course and now, as twilight settled across the Sky and the air cooled again, *The Siren* sailed toward them.

"They're coming." Nicholas pointed to some of the crew climbing into the jolly boat. "Getting the jolly back on the lift out here won't be fun."

She looked at the jolly boat preparing to descend and her heart did a flip to rival a mermaid when her mother climbed into the little boat, her thick, dark braid draped over her shoulder.

"Do you honestly care?" Hannah laughed, happiness spilling out of her like water out of a sieve.

"Not in the slightest." Nicholas smirked before shifting to sit on one fish rather than stretch out across the two like Hannah.

"Thanks for the ride." He patted the Cuddler's head. "You two make a decent raft."

The fish chirped and Hannah swore it sounded annoyed.

She shifted to mirror Nicholas and patted the Cuddler that saved her on its head. "Thank you. We'd be dead without you."

Her fish chirped and nuzzled its head against her hand, almost like it would miss her.

"Hannah! Nicholas!"

Hannah couldn't stop the tears that pressed against her eyes as she caught sight of their parents rowing toward them.

Their rescue party had arrived.

Her exhaustion hit as soon as her father and Matthew pulled her into the jolly.

"Mother Land, Sea, and Sky, I thought I'd never see you again!" Her mother held her tighter than *The Siren*'s stays held its masts.

Hannah clung to her mother, vaguely aware of Nicholas reuniting with his own parents. As her father wrapped both her and her mother in his arms, the two days and full night spent adrift crashed down on Hannah, and she collapsed beneath the weight.

"We've got you." Her father kissed her head. "We've got you."

The jolly boat required four oarsmen, so Hannah's parents transferred her to Nicholas's side and started back for the ship. Hannah leaned into him. Every part of her body cried out in exhaustion, but her heart sent out a silent prayer of gratitude to the Three Sisters. Hannah had a life again, a life that she could live with Nicholas, a life that could include all the things she thought hours ago she'd never have. She hoped Edith would let them stay with her while they got their feet under them. Hannah wanted to set up in the same city as Edith. If she couldn't have her mother there when she started having children, Edith was the next best thing.

Nicholas rested his head against hers, and Hannah smiled. They would sit, just like this, but not in a jolly boat in the middle of the Sea. They would sit in front of a fire in a cozy little home, and she would have a baby, their baby, wrapped in her arms.

Getting the jolly back on the lift interrupted her daydream. The open water required the efforts of all six of them, and Hannah's muscles cried out in protest as she helped get all the lift ropes into place.

"The last hurdle and then we're home." Nicholas encouraged her with a tired smile. "If we're lucky, we won't see a Nerland ship till morning."

"If we see a Nerland ship in the morning, I'll lock myself in the brig." Hannah chuckled as they got the lift ropes in place around the jolly. Her mother's whistle gave the call to bring them up.

"Can I join you?" Nicholas winked at her.

"Neither of you will join any fights till you're rested and have some water and food." Rebecca's stern glare struck Hannah as funny, and she laughed harder.

"But Mother." Nicholas sank next to Hannah. "You wouldn't suggest we be rude to our guests, would you? The least we can do is offer the courtesy of being killed by whichever member of the crew they'd like."

Hannah gripped her sides as she laughed. Her chest ached from the effort, but she didn't care. This was her happy ending. Everything would be perfect. And it would all start the moment they touched the deck. She was going to climb out of the jolly and kiss Nicholas for the entire crew to see and then she wanted a cool drink and her bunk.

She held onto the side of the jolly boat and smiled as they rose into the air.

Hannah took Captain Roberts's hand as they reached the main deck and she climbed back onto *The Siren*. The warmth from being high above the waves pulled some of the ache from her muscles and she smiled as the captain wrapped her in a hug.

"Do me a favor and don't jump ship when we're trying to escape a monster." He chuckled and smiled down at her before Anthony pulled her away and into his own embrace.

"Land and Sky, Hannah! It was bad enough to watch Nicholas fall overboard, but watching you jump..."

Anthony choked on his next word and held her tighter. Hannah squeezed her arms around him. She looked up to reassure him she was fine when Nicholas joined their hug.

"Don't worry, mate." Nicholas said as Anthony shifted to pull him into the hug. "I'm never leaving *The Siren* again."

Six words.

Six words said with finality, with relief.

Six words that broke all the hope Hannah had moments ago.

She would have Nicholas, but nothing else. She would lose every other dream.

Hannah pulled away from the hug, dizzy and nauseated as her dreams of children and a life of peace shattered around her. Her vision clouded with dark spots as a buzzing sound filled her ears. She dropped to the deck and held her head between her knees. The dark spots grew larger, just like *The Siren* had on the horizon, tempting Hannah to give into the blackness that beckoned her. Life wasn't fair—for a pirate, especially. Why would her second chance at life be anything more than a second chance?

Then the smell of Nicholas flooded her as he cradled her in his arms and lifted her from the deck. The shouting of unintelligible voices flooded her ears, and she curled further into Nicholas, ready to embrace the darkness tugging on her.

"Stay with us, Hannah." His voice pulled her back, holding more than concern. It held the reminder of her promise to him.

She told him she wanted more. How could she go back on that now? After everything they'd come through, two days adrift in the Sea, the secrets they shared, the intimacy between them now, how could she walk away?

Her heart broke. Hannah could never walk away from him. Not now. Not knowing that he wanted her as much as she wanted him. Shame filled her. How could she ask for something she knew he couldn't give her? It wasn't fair to him, for her to ask him to give up everything for a silly dream, a dream she'd known from the beginning was a long shot. This was her second chance at life. She should be grateful, even if her second chance at life came with the death of all but one of her dreams.

Then a cup pressed against her lips, as cold as her new reality, and the water as bitter as the ashes of her dead dreams. But she drank, because the thought alone of losing both Nicholas and her dream of a family with him threatened to drown her. The smell of healing smoke wrapped around Hannah and her mother's frantic prayer to Mother Land filled her ears. The healing power of Mother Land wouldn't help. Smoke and prayers were for broken bones, not broken hearts.

Hannah swallowed the water with her tears. She'd known from the beginning she'd lose a part of her heart. She best let this part die, and hope she could learn to live with what remained.

Chapter Ten
Hide And Seek

Nicholas crept to the galley. The full night's sleep after their rescue gave him back some of his edge as he kept in the shadows. He pressed his back against the wall, breathing slowly, the air scratching against his lungs. A consequence of putting his own healing off the night before to ensure Hannah was all right. He waited ten heartbeats before jumping into the galley.

And right into Anthony.

Anthony swore as he caught himself from falling against the stove.

"What in Land's name is going on?"

Nicholas rubbed his hand over his face and groaned at his blunder. "I thought you were Hannah."

"I thought she was still sleeping." Anthony grabbed the dried fish he'd dropped from the floor. He broke it in half and handed a piece to Nicholas.

"She wasn't there when I checked thirty minutes ago." Nicholas bit down on the fish and let the salt fill his mouth before adding, "I think she's hiding from me again."

Anthony looked up at the ceiling and uttered several more curses.

"My sentiments exactly." Nicholas moved to lean against the counter, gripping the smooth wood. "She was distant last night, but I blamed it on her collapsing when we climbed aboard."

"Was she distant while you two were adrift? She couldn't very well hide from you there."

Nicholas dropped his head to his chest and pushed away the terrifying thought that Hannah might regret what they'd said to each other while floating on their Speckled Chirper raft.

"No. Honestly, I thought we had figured a lot of that out while we were floating in the waves."

"Do I need to offer congratulations?" Anthony elbowed him in the ribs with a grin.

"Apparently not, seeing as she's hiding from me again. Mother Land and Sky, what did I do?"

"You two are going to drive me mad." Anthony shoved off of the counter. "I'll go find her."

"No." Nicholas grabbed Anthony's arm. "I'm going to find her and I'm going to figure this out. I'm not giving up until she tells me to."

"Well then." Anthony grinned and squeezed his shoulder. "If I see her, I'll let you know which way she went. *The Siren* isn't that big. She can't hide from you forever."

"That's my hope."

As Nicholas returned to his search, he conceded that Hannah might not be able to hide from him forever, but the woman hid better than anyone he knew. He searched each deck meticulously, coming up empty-handed after every sweep. The only bright side was that the awful heat had dissipated and didn't suffocate him every time he descended below deck. For a terrifying moment while he searched, Nicholas feared she had fallen overboard again. However, Alice and David assured him they'd seen their daughter within the last hour when he'd asked. Of course, Hannah wasn't where they said when Nicholas went back to investigate.

An errant idea crossed his mind that perhaps Hannah was playing, giving them something to do since Captain Roberts excused them from work for the next week. If that was the case, he could think of plenty of better things to distract them from a week without chores. But Nicholas knew in his heart that it wasn't so simple, and even if he had to hide in her bunk tonight, he'd find her.

He descended the stairs to check the galley again when the whistle call for an approaching Nerland naval ship sounded. Nicholas groaned, instinct driving through him as he turned to run back up the stairs. But then Hannah's words echoed in his mind.

If we see a Nerlander ship in the morning, I'll lock myself in the brig.

It was late afternoon now, but maybe she was serious. Nicholas turned back, heading for the stairs down to the hold and the brig.

He refused to let her get away. Whatever Hannah needed from him, Nicholas determined right there he'd move the Sea, Sky, and Mother Land to get it for her. He was hers, and he planned to make that as clear as water—as soon as he found her.

Chapter Eleven
Living, For Real This Time

Hannah sat next to one of the two cells in the brig, both filled to the brim with supplies. She shouldn't be in here, but hiding from Nicholas was proving harder than she thought. Last time—Sea and Sky, it had only been three days ago—Nicholas hadn't pursued her so relentlessly. But today, he was after her like a crab after a new shell. It was exhausting. She'd come to the brig, hoping it was so far out of the way, unused as it was, that she'd be safe to rest for a moment.

Hannah needed to keep away long enough for her heart to mourn her dreams of leaving *The Siren* and having children of her own. Once she could accept that, she could face Nicholas and try to live again.

The whistle of a ship sighting drifted above her and Hannah shot to her feet. Her muscles screamed at the action. She grabbed the bars beside her as her vision went black for a heart stopping moment. The sound of heavy tread echoed and Hannah panicked that her sight wouldn't return before the steps reached her.

The black cleared and as light and color flooded her vision, Hannah looked up to see Nicholas run into the brig.

"Finally." His breathing heaved as he sank down to the floor.

"Why haven't you had someone heal you?" Hannah dropped to his side, wishing she had a candle. "You can't run when your breathing sounds like that!"

He coughed through his answer.

"I had...to get...to you." He coughed harder and his shoulders rose and fell like driftwood in the waves.

If guilt wasn't eating her alive already, it was now.

"Oh, Nicholas." Hannah wrapped her arms around him, hating that he'd put off his own healing because she'd hid.

It was all such a mess. She hadn't wanted to hurt Nicholas. He'd given no hint that he'd leave *The Siren* for her. In fact, he'd always said he'd never leave. It was her own stupid heart that had hoped that she could have it all. Hannah believed that with time, being with him would be enough. She would be happy. She just needed some space to come to terms with reality.

"Why are you," he panted, "hiding from me?"

Hannah handed Nicholas her waterskin, rubbing his back as he worked to regain control of his breathing.

"It's not your fault." She answered when his breathing mellowed.

"That's not what I asked." Nicholas hooked her waterskin back on her belt and grabbed her hand. He held on tight, like he was afraid she'd run. "I told you I wanted more, and I meant it. Our rescue didn't change that."

"I know." Hannah kept her eyes on his hand wrapped around hers.

"Did it change for you?"

Nicholas's words cut through Hannah's heart. The guilt that her heart wasn't happy with only him was bad enough, but knowing that he worried she'd changed her mind about him left her drowning in the pain.

"No, Nicholas, I..." She stopped as the whistle call to battle stations sounded from the main deck.

"Leave them. They'll send us back here if we try to help." He reached for Hannah and she let him pull her up into his arms. Nicholas pushed up from the floor and

Hannah let him pull her up into his arms. He tucked a stray lock behind her ear and leaned in close. "Do you want me?"

"I do." Hannah breathed him in. She'd missed this. Missed being wrapped in his arms. Missed how her whole body gave into him when he was this close.

"And I want you." He rested his forehead against hers. "So, what's the problem?"

The cannons fired above them, rocking the ship and sending the couple back against the planks. Nicholas's arm caught the wall behind her, forcing Hannah to stare up at him. For a moment, she wished he had pinned her against the wall and kissed her.

Then she remembered his question, and those thoughts rushed out like the tide. "Don't hate me."

"I'll grow a merman's tail instead of legs before I hate you."

She prayed he was right. "I want something I can't have, and I need time to get past it. I'm not upset with you and I promise if you give me that time..."

"What do you want?" Nicholas cut her off. "Whatever it is, I'll get it, I'll find it."

Frustration boiled in her stomach at his promise as the cannons fired again.

"But you won't! You said yourself you'll never leave *The Siren*! And I can't have a family of my own if we stay!" The ship turned sharply and Hannah grabbed Nicholas's shirt to keep herself upright. "So forgive me if I need time to come to terms with the fact that I'll never have children with the man that I love!"

"You want a family?" His eyes went wide, but Hannah didn't miss the slightest upturn at the left corner of his mouth.

"Aye." Hannah shoved against his chest, but he boxed her in. "And letting that go is harder than I expected."

"Don't." Nicholas stepped closer, pinning her against the wall. "Don't let it go. We'll figure something out."

"We can't both leave the ship." She shook her head, the dying part of her heart slowly fading into its afterlife.

"We'll talk to the Merfolk. I'll bring Anthony and the Sea in if we need to, but we'll find a way."

"What if we can't?" Hannah tangled her fingers back in his shirt as the cannons fired again.

"Did you honestly think I'd be able to stay here if you left?" Nicholas's hand moved to her cheek and he leaned in closer. "I've already come up with plenty of options to get two people off this ship."

The dying part of her heart shuddered back to life, beating as though it had never lost the will to live.

"You'd leave *The Siren*? For me?"

Nicholas shook his head. "Not for you, with you. I've loved you since I was fifteen. Now that I know you love me, I'm with you forever."

Hannah closed the space between them, capturing his lips with her kiss as the cannons fired again. There were no guarantees, but knowing that Nicholas would leave with her if the opportunity presented itself was enough. She was alive, and if the Three Sisters saw fit to not block every path Nicholas had thought of, she'd have every dream her heart had hoped for.

"I love you." Hannah pulled back, lowering back down to the floor.

"And I love you." Nicholas smiled, then brought his lips back to hers.

His fingers threaded through the base of her braid, and Hannah fumbled to undo the tie as she tried to not break their kiss. He pressed against her, his hands cradling her head as her hair fell from its tie and Hannah unraveled with it. Her hands pulled his shirt from his pants, desperate to feel his skin beneath her fingers again. Nicholas pulled back long enough to throw his shirt over his head before he brought his lips to her neck.

Warmth radiated from his chest, and Hannah traced every curve and divot of muscle as his hands wandered from her hair, caressing every part of her.

Nicholas pulled his lips to her ear, his breathing as heavy as the tread of footsteps.

Footsteps?

"For Land's sake!" Anthony yelled.

Hannah gasped and curled into Nicholas's chest as Anthony turned his back to them.

Nicholas groaned. "Anthony, wait."

"No, no, I can see you didn't hear the fighting stop. The Nerlanders are on the bottom of the Sea. I'm thrilled for you both. Goodbye!"

Anthony's hurried steps faded, and Hannah couldn't stop her laughter.

"Sky and Sea, that wasn't how I wanted him to find us." Nicholas dropped his head to her shoulder.

"It could be worse." Hannah tangled her fingers in his hair. "He could have found us with both our shirts off."

"Fair." Nicholas chuckled before turning to kiss her neck. "We should probably go up. Anthony is too good a friend to say anything, but the rest of the crew will know something is going on when we don't show up on deck with him."

"Aye." Hannah sighed, not wanting to stop, but Nicholas was right, and being found by Anthony was bad enough. She did not want her father finding her in this state.

Nicholas stepped back and picked up his shirt, sliding it over his head. Hannah found her hair tie but didn't bother to braid her hair again.

"Can I tell you something?" Nicholas pulled her back to him, running his hands through her loose waves.

"Anything." Hannah traced the line of his neck to his shoulder with a soft smile. Everything was right between them.

"When you're ready, I'm going to marry you, Hannah Vallens."

Hannah's smile grew to aching. "I'm ready!" She grabbed his hand and ran for the main deck.

"What?" Nicholas stopped her, wrapping his arms around her waist, pulling her close.

"You said when I'm ready. I'm ready to be Hannah Ainsley. Let's go tell Captain Roberts he's performing a wedding."

"Now? You're sure?"

Hannah pressed up and gave him a quick kiss. "I'm done waiting for my dreams to come to me. I'm ready to be yours."

Nicholas kissed her, his smile breaking it too soon. "Aye, we've wasted enough time, I suppose."

The only thing keeping Hannah from flying up to the main deck was Nicholas's hand holding hers. Coming out into the sun, a cool breeze wrapped around them, and Hannah breathed it in. Even the weather knew it was time for change, the best kind of change.

"Captain!" Hannah called when she caught sight of Captain Roberts near the helm.

"Aye, Hannah."

"Marry us!"

She laughed at the captain's blank stare.

"Hannah?" Her mother ran to her side, her father, Rebecca and Matthew not far behind. "What are you talking about?"

Hannah smiled up at Nicholas, who looked to be putting a great deal of effort into not laughing. "I'm getting married."

"Aye, I heard that, but why right now?"

"Because I'm done waiting. Nicholas and I have loved each other for years, Mother."

"We all knew that, dear, but why not put on a nice dress? And let us braid your hair?" Alice took the tie from Hannah's hands.

"And Nicholas should change too." Rebecca reached up, trying to fix Nicholas's hair that Hannah had put a great deal of effort into mussing.

"None of that matters to me." Hannah hugged her mother. "I'm happy, just like this."

"Let them have it, Alice." David wrapped his arm around Alice's shoulders. "If we'd been in different circumstances, we would have done the same thing."

"You're sure?" Rebecca took Hannah's hand. "You never get your wedding back."

"I'm sure." Hannah hugged Rebecca, smiling at the crew gathering around. "I love your son. I don't need anything else."

"That's good enough for me." Matthew joined the hug.

"We have our parents's approval, then?" Nicholas laughed as both his mother and Alice turned to glare at him.

"Aye, we'll be glad to be here for it." David clapped Nicholas on the shoulder and Hannah smiled.

"Thank you, David." Nicholas turned to Captain Roberts. "What do you say, Captain? Can you spare us a few minutes?"

"Aye, to the poop deck with you." Captain Roberts smiled before bringing his whistle to his lips.

The call for all hands on deck had never brought Hannah so much joy.

She took Nicholas's hand and together they ran to the poop deck.

She was getting married!

Captain Roberts's ceremony was wonderful. Hannah was sure it was. But she didn't hear a word of it. Her parents stood behind her, Nicholas's parents stood behind him, and Anthony stood at his side, but Nicholas held the whole of her attention. Their days adrift were distant memories now, Edith's offer a faint whisper from another life. Pledging her life to Nicholas, knowing he wanted the same things for their future as she did, was all that mattered.

"Kiss her, Nicholas." The captain's voice broke through Hannah's thoughts. "She deserves it after all the two of you have gone through."

Hannah didn't have a chance to respond to the captain's teasing. Nicholas pulled her close, threading his fingers through her loose waves, and kissed her like a man with a second chance at life.

A second chance that Hannah couldn't wait to live out with him.

Chapter Twelve

Epilogue

One Month Later

Nicholas grinned when his gentle caressing finally stirred his sleeping wife. She blinked up at him; the sunlight filtering into their hut on *The Siren's* protected island in the Mer Sea. He loved how the light highlighted the red in her brown hair. She was still red, still determined in everything she did.

"Good morning." He kissed her shoulder and smiled as she yawned.

"Good morning." She arched as she stretched, and Nicholas shifted closer to her. "I hope you slept as well as I did."

"Aye, our bed is much nicer than the bunks on the ship." He moved his fingers from her arm to her bare shoulder.

"Really? I had no idea you enjoyed this more." Hannah smirked up at him and Nicholas thanked the Sea, Sky and Mother Land she was his.

"I'll have to do a better job at showing you than I did last night."

Hannah smiled and sighed as his hands wandered. Her fingers tangled in the hair at the base of neck, pulling him down to her kiss.

"We should make sure the stowaway didn't escape from Anthony's hut and find out if the Sea told him what we're supposed to do with her." She murmured when he pulled back.

"We would have heard Captain's call by now if she escaped. Let Anthony handle her. We're not close enough to the Merfolk or the Sea to have any sway in it." Nicholas deepened his kiss, sliding against her until her breath caught. "Besides, no one is expecting us to come out of here for the foreseeable future. Maggie joked she'd have our meals left at our door."

"At some point, I want my questions about her answered." She arched into his hand as he ran it down her side. "But I suppose you can show me how much more you like our bed than the ship's bunks first." Hannah's teeth grazed his lip before sliding her hands from his neck to trace his chest.

Nicholas chased her lips. "Now you've got the right idea of it."

Thank You!

Dear Reader,

Thank you so much for reading *Love, Ships & Sea Serpents*! If you enjoyed it, I'd really appreciate a review on your preferred retailer. It helps other readers discover this little book of mine. ♥

And if you don't want to miss out on Anthony's story, make sure you go to https://elainecanyon.com/love-mystique-mermaids to get your copy of *Love, Mystique & Mermaids*! Anthony's going to find out how meddlesome the Sea really is—especially when she's decided she's a matchmaker.

Till then,

Elaine ♥

Kickstarter Pirate Crew

Thank you to all the backers of the *Love, Mystique & Mermaids* Kickstarter campaign! Your support not only made sure that Anthony and Marissa's story happened, you also made sure Nicholas and Hannah received the same extra special treatment. I'm incredibly honored you let me stand as your captain during the campaign. You are and always will be my crew.

R Sarty

Gabrielle Landi

Chriss Romney

E. R. Paskey

Ashley

Nicolle Morock

Laura Nelson

Liza Clarke

Gianna Christopher

Nicole Wright

Amanda Thompson

J.L. Hendricks

M.E. Cooper

Christy S

J.S. Lawson

Abby Bontreger

K.Q. Kimler

Emma

Cortney Babcock

Ashley D.

Erika G.

Carol MacLennan-Gonzales

Kay Leyda

Emerald Bruce

Nalamba

Mellissa

Ashley

Emeraldragonlady

Madeleine Wijono

Nicole Folsom

Molly Fessel

Jonathon Mast

Moni

Belinda Kroll

Franchesca Caram

Katelyn Hester

K. S. Gerlt

Jocelyn Lindsay

Zilla

crispy

Alexis

Holly D. Morgan

Scarlett

Amy Trent

Allee Snyder

Elizabeth Ansley

Valentine Jauner

Kathy Gordon

Marlene

Sunny Ryan

Florentina

Garrie Powers

L Barr

Kimmi Irvine

Heather G Harris

@becksreadingbooks

Lynn P.

Ana Lewis

Claire Kohler

Kai'lee

Valerie Anne

Amanda Balter

A. Reece

Shaelei

Anna Daley

Charlotte U. P.

Taylor Maris

Amanda Eschmeyer

Ember Mae

Lara Adrienne

Katherine Malloy

Samantha Nicole Newberry

Leigh Romero

Amanda Hill

Kathryn Maris

Tania L

Ivy Ru

Jessica Hoppe

R. Johnson

Kaylen - Your Write or Die

Alexandra Corrsin

Keri K

Kristen Schleif

C

Savannah Coats

Rebecca P

J.D. Penndagger

Morgan G.

Stef

Carissa Boehmer

R Hagberg

Rachael Barcellano

Jessica Armstrong

Dana

Hannah Lozano

Karina Krogh

Midnightmare

Liana

Sleepy Panda

Pauline Beltran

Tahlia, with love. -Jamie

And everyone else!

"I want more too." His low voice rolled through her like the incoming tide. "I wanted more and I want more."

Acknowledgements

To quote Mel Brooks, I'll say what's in my heart. Ba-bump. Ba-bump. Ba-bump.

But in all seriousness, this book wouldn't be here without the help of so many.

First, I'd like to thank my husband, children, and family, who all have supported me on this crazy journey from writing serialized fanfiction to this book today. I love you!

Second, thank you to my fanfiction friends, who cheered me through every fic regardless of the ship I wrote, and who still cheer me on. I love you, ladies!

Thank you to my beta readers. Your help was invaluable.

Thank you to the Authortuber community, especially S.D. Huston, who welcomed me with open arms, support, and guidance anytime I remembered to ask.

Thank you to the Fictionary company and community. All of you were crucial to my growth as an author and building my confidence to hit publish.

Again, thank you to all the Kickstarter backers of the *Love, Mystique & Mermaids* campaign.

And you, dear reader, thank you for sailing these seas with me.

Also By Elaine Canyon

Love & A Bit of Disorder

~Outcasts of Nerland~
Love, Ships & Sea Serpents
Love, Mystique & Mermaids
Love, Discretion & Dragons

~The Virdinra Chronicles~
Love, Dryads & Murder

~Adapted Tales~
Love, Cinder & Slippers

About the Author

Elaine Canyon writes Romantasy Comedies, because you shouldn't have to choose between a romantasy and a rom-com. Her books feature closed-door romances in bright fantasy worlds with characters that are sure to leave you laughing. Elaine lives in the mountains of central Utah with her husband and children, all of whom she loves dearly. When she's not writing, you can find her in the mountains, hiking, rock climbing, and skiing with her family.

www.ingramcontent.com/pod-product-compliance
Lightning Source LLC
Chambersburg PA
CBHW071428300726
48976CB00004B/1268